NEW AGE GOTHIC

Witch Soul

Cover art by Andie Lugtu

ISBN: 978-1-7331699-4-3

Content Warnings

Mentions of past self-harm
Body dysmorphia
Past malnourishment and trauma while in prison
Past emotional abuse from a parent
General bloody vampire violence

This is a romance novel for adults, and it involves explicit sex. If you don't like reading this, please be warned.

Also in the New Age Gothic series
A Flame in the Night

Praise for *A Flame in the Night*

"I absolutely loved this book. The prose is beautiful. The characters are complex. Every bit of this book drips decadence and eroticism and I ate it up. I was so sad to see it end because I wanted to spend so much more time with the characters. This is the vampire book the queers deserve."
- Luna Fiore, author of *Unbound*

"Sexy, decadent, a delight."
- Ladz, author of *Ice Upon A Pier*

Chapter 1

Millie

Quite frankly, Millie's never had the best luck, but prison is a new low.

Sentenced to thirty years on a bullshit charge—illegally selling prescription drugs? Yeah. Maybe it's actually a new high, now that she thinks about it. High on the chart of "good work fucking up your life."

The last letter from Mom said as much.

I never want to hear from you again.

Back on a lumpy mattress, Millie trails her fingers over the scars on her cheek.

She never *sold* anything, technically. Especially not prescription drugs, but her crime unprecedented: a fledgling witch trying to alchemically manipulate an element, now often used in negligible doses in beauty products, to find a way to stop the mysterious gaunt outbreak among vampires.

What else can Azoth, a natural alchemical component of life itself, found in anything from ant trails to the ghosts of butterfly wings, be but a highly regulated medicine?

If Millie were to give out her results, the potential cure, she would've done it for free, which seems to many even more questionable and inexcusable—because who the hell gives out medicine to the sick and desperate without expecting compensation? Surely, it's more immoral to do all that effort for free than to charge eight-hundred dollars a bottle.

Six months into a mind-numbing prison routine, Millie thinks that she might lose her mind. She thinks about her childhood. She misses the smell of her home basement, of aloe, mint, lavender, and rosemary. She misses drinking lemon balm tea with Granny on the front porch and watching the hummingbirds dance around a feeder.

Curling on the mattress,, stomach roiling from the soggy rolls and watery cranberry sauce she ate last night, Millie stands and wanders out of her spartan dorm, barely passing a glance to the guards who follows her, as she looks in her floor's small, square break room, the only place she eats outside of the food hall.

The old microwave reads *7:26* in the evening. Time for work; maybe it'll take her mind off her stomach. She lolls her head to the side. Her neck pops, and she winces; her back is a tight, aching coil.

More often than not, her mind is slower. She often forgets why she's walked into a room.

Normally in the mornings, she eats plain oatmeal, with only enough water that most of it isn't gritty dusty crunching between her teeth. Sometimes, they're allowed eggs and two pieces of toast, which both have the texture of rubber. For lunch and dinner, there's a lot of beans, potatoes, and soup, with the occasional semi-cooked chicken wings or hamburgers. She's lost thirty-six pounds since she was incarcerated.

When they're allowed some time to themselves, the women in her dorm might indulge in potato vodka. The only break from the monotony is the prison library, but since finishing one dark fantasy series and *The Eye of the World*, even reading feels dull and listless.

She's dull and listless. Her pale skin is sickly white, all except for the blue bruises under her eyes. Other prisoners get visitors; she doesn't. She can't vote. Won't be able to get a decent job if they ask about her criminal history, which they will.

She works, she eats, she sleeps, she shits, and she looks at the same gray walls all day. Is she even Millie anymore?

Was she ever?

Mom's blazing hazel eyes, bright with fury and disappointment; but thinking on it, Millie can't remember a time when they ever shone with pride.

Go on, then. If you won't respect me. If you insist on embarrassing us and letting the whole neighborhood—my friends—know you're a dyke. Millie had been so morose and wondering what she should've done differently to please her mother that she couldn't bring herself to correct her and say, *Well, bisexual.*

When Millie stands numbly at the snack vending machines, she sets her fingers on the cool surface and feels the faint buzz inside her, but her powers have always been more in alchemy than in casting spells.

If only she learned to tame her witch soul, maybe she'd be powerful.

The only thing she has to herself is her hair, tangled and limp; turns out, shaving prisoners bald is old-fashioned.

She heads to the end of the dorm hall to start her job, hoping to be done before ten. For nineteen dollars a month—yes, the entire month—she sweeps and cleans the floor, including the game room, empty at this late hour.

The same floor, the same walls, the same voices and laughs of people as wary and weary as her. Her thoughts circle and circle like sharks catching a whiff of chum.

"Stir-crazy" doesn't begin to describe it.

Millie thinks, *I won't give up. If I give up on myself, who else is left? Who else can find the cure and actually put it to good purpose without making people break the bank?*

Hour by hour, day by day. Keep going.

All I have is myself.

All I deserve is myself.

The witch soul inside her doesn't contradict her.

Normally, a single guard watches her, but since she's proven herself to be weak, she's had more than one play on their phone while she cleans, or occasionally engage in small talk about things happening outside.

Curfews. More people wearing silver, which only helps with weaker gaunts and starving vampires. Arguments over how to keep the "good vampires" from turning, and then the putrid rabbithole of conspiracy theories.

As Millie carries the broom, she doesn't look much at the guard, who has the usual disinterested look on a long and narrow face. While Millie wears dull blue, long-sleeved scrubs, the guard wears a light gray collared shirt, and slate gray slacks, ribbed by a belt holding a stun gun and pepper spray; only guards in the observation towers have weapons, since waltzing around with guns and batons around the prison populace increases the risk of an inmate seizing them.

The game room is a gray square with dim lighting, like the rest of the dorm. A well-worn pool table lounges in the center.

On the leftmost side of the room is a 2005 square TV on a near-barren wooden stand with a PS2 and GameCube, with only three games available. Most games in the prison come from tablets the inmates check out for a fee.

Millie always liked playing video games when she was a kid, ever since she raised her chubby fist in rage when her five-year-old brain couldn't tell why the stupid bear with a monocle wouldn't drop the bridge for her to pass. Her ex-boyfriend Simon would play anything from *Mario* to *Dark Souls* with her; she got madder at *Mario*.

But now what she wants most is some music and at least one right earbud. God. Would it kill them to let her listen to a *little* Cradle of Filth every now and again? She'd just have to ensure the song titles the guards saw were the poetic ones and not, say, "Gilded Cunt" or "Lord Abortion."

"You look so different," the guard murmurs.

Millie looks at the other woman out of the corner of her eye. "Sorry, were you talking to me?"

The guard wiggles her nose in a cute way that reminds Millie of an ex-girlfriend. "I'm so sorry we weren't able to come sooner. We weren't sure if we could pull it off, so we planned and practiced. Way too long."

Millie furtively stares as a dust bunny rolls on the ground like a tumbleweed. "What?" The guard has her cap well over her face, her hair in a brunette ponytail, but when Millie looks closer.

Wait.

A glamor—no, a physically shifted form; a shifter, one of the people descended from the sidhe, with a variety of different kinds of shapeshifters and changelings, including faoladh, who are essentially werewolves who protect people. Though many sidhe can be monstrous, like humans, the faoladh are fixated on helping and guarding others.

And with her attuned sensitivity to the supernatural, Millie narrows her eyes and sees a woman with a body like a wire, taller than she appears—about a head taller than Millie, who barely scratches five feet—with frost-blue eyes and silvery blonde hair in long, wild curls, her skin a cool olive tone. On her narrow face, a jagged scar spiders from her jaw to her right cheekbone, high and cutting as glass.

Millie's expression softens, her eyes burning. "Fel?"

Reminds her of an ex-girlfriend. Yes. *This* ex-girlfriend.

"Yeah." Fel sniffs and grimaces, her voice raspy but warm. "Those pieces of Thanksgiving turkey were not done at *all.*"

Millie offers a watery smile. "There's a reason I've almost become a vegetarian here." She sucks in a breath through her nose; she *won't* be a huge pansy and cry. She hasn't cried for all the days she's been here, so why start now? "You know, this might be the first time I've seen you without flannel on. Flannel shirts, flannel boxers..."

Before she knows it, Fel lurches forward and pulls Millie into a tight hug. Millie's shoulders ache, and she clumsily returns the hug and inhales the scents of fur, earth, and citrus mouthwash.

When they break apart, Fel still has her hands on Millie's shoulders, and when Millie takes one of them to hold, she sees that translucent bed of hair atop Fel's hand. "What are you doing here? Don't tell me you've been working here as a guard the entire time."

Fel blinks and snorts. "Huh? No. I'm busting you out. You know, I've been practicing my invisibility."

Millie blinks, too. Her heart constricts.

Someone cares about you enough to save you.

She must be mistaken.

That's not her witch soul's voice. It's her.

Fel looks around, as if expecting someone to be snooping. "Come on, Mills, let's go, before you're missed."

Missed. Right.

Millie's throat squeezes, and her hope suddenly curdles into anxiety as she follows Fel into the hall. "Where exactly are we going to, you know, do this?"

A pause. "Out."

"Out," Millie repeats. "Right. Good."

Fel has always been a fly by the seat of your pants non-planner, spontaneous, and Millie has never known how to accommodate that. Without a schedule in advance for social visits, she gets grumpy and tired fast.

I could be free tonight, and then...

And then.

I'm going to eat the meanest grilled cheese with hot tomato soup ever.

The idea makes her stomach cramp, but she looks forward to it.

"Simon'll be waiting for us," Fel tells her, looking over her shoulder, their hands still locked together as they briskly race down the stairs.

Millie swallows thickly. "Simon, he..."

"Yeah, he's got the car parked a few blocks away. We can cut through the woods. Let's go."

Simon and Felicity. It's not every day your exes get together; and it's especially not every day they team up to break you out of prison.

They didn't forget her.

Of course they didn't.

I'm so stupid. So cynical. Shame on you, you idiot.

Millie says as they reach a landing, "Right. Better now than later."

That's when she loses sight of Fel and their joined hands.

Chapter 2

Millie expected that it'd be rather hard to run out of the prison, even while invisible at night. After all, they still have to open doors and such and hope no one wonders why doors are moving by themselves.

And, as they sneak out of the dorms and enter the prison proper, a gloom settles over the quiet, gray hall where only a cobweb sways in the ceiling corner.

At first, the single noise is rain, which feels a country away. She tries to listen to footsteps, while though they're both invisible, she can feel the twists in Fel's muscles as her head darts toward the softest, distant sounds that Millie can't hear, even with her good ear.

They press against the cold walls as guards pass by, yawning and palming for their phones. As they glide past rows and rows of doors, one opens, and they both lurch away from it and seize to a stop, so still that Millie isn't sure if she's breathing when a guard and another prisoner, holding a mop, head toward the cafeteria. Whereas Fel has always been lithe, Millie's lack of doing and saying much for six months makes her sluggish.

Tense and waiting for an alarm, Millie expects for them to be detected, especially near the security gates where the room they bleed into looks more like a doctor's office with wall mail slots than a prison. Three narrow rows of black chairs; white walls in contrast with all the gray, and an entrance desk, also painted white where a generic screensaver dances on a Windows 8 computer screen. She blinks at the amount of lights, and a guard sitting in front of the desktop plays Solitaire on her phone.

"Wait," she whispers to Fel, getting an idea as she looks back at one of the ajar doors in the hall. She sneaks to the door and peeks inside, only to hear faint snoring.

"What are we doing?" Fel asks her when Millie slowly, silently opens the door. Bingo.

Inside the room is an asleep guard with crossed arms, and a styrofoam cup of coffee sits precariously near a computer panel and a series of camera footage on this single floor.

Every prison block has a guard post with a console that has two small, red "open all cell doors" buttons that must be pressed simultaneously, so prisoners can flee to safety quickly in case of a fire.

She should've started doing this before; these buttons will only open all the cell doors in a single block.

She tells Fel this.

"Won't that trigger an alarm?" Fel asks.

"No. It'll just free some of the prisoners. This is usually here in case there *is* an alarm. Prisoners don't get released every time an alarm goes off."

"Oh, good thinking. If other people are running around, the chaos might be a distraction."

That's not why I'm doing it, Millie thinks but doesn't say. If the correctional officers had guns, she wouldn't do it, but she knows that they're underpaid, understaffed, and unarmed. Her own struggles have made her selfish and not as attuned to anyone else's pain, but she could at least do this.

She presses down on both buttons for about five seconds. On one of the camera feeds, the cell doors open, most of the inmates wander toward the open doors in bleary confusion, but two of the women make a break for it. Others, most, look out into the hall, as if determining whether it's worth it, or where they'll go.

Then, Millie takes Fel's hand again, and they run.

Like fluid, they're past the front entrance metal detectors and out the door. A shock of cold rakes through Millie, tumbling down her shoulders and alighting her sore back with a chilly tingle.

Her mind whirs, hand slick with sweat, but neither she nor Fel lose hold of one another. Goosebumps rise under her sleeves, her senses so acute now that she feels the friction of small hairs on her arm grazing against the cloth. Her head spins when she feels a cool plop of rain on her nose; she has rarely been allowed outside.

Despite the near-blinding lights outside, the rain and shadows give her the impression of endless darkness. She wants to ask Fel where they'll go once they dive into the woods. What if they get lost? What if they lose one another?

In the bright lights, the front prison gate gives the impression of a high—impossibly high—and narrow face with curlicue hair. That, or the mockery of a window with its crossing gray lines.

Thankfully, the entrance is wide open as a small trail of bulky vehicles surge into the yard. That's right. Especially with a witch in the prison, albeit a stunted one, the deliveries tend to take place at night any time before three-thirty, when the first prisoners are awakened.

Even then, the guards are lethargic and distracted. Millie hopes that's enough.

As they stand on the autumn-blunted grass, the air flooding with shouts and orders that she swears will turn against her, Millie squeezes Fel's hand, and her invisible friend squeezes back.

Never before has Millie realized her utter fear of being seen.

Fingers an entwined, almost painful knot in the biting cold, they run for it.

Her lungs shrivel and paradoxically feel so swollen that they'll burst as they run past the gate and hulking vehicles and begin to ascend a series of hills that melt into the woods. The wintry scent of frosted pines crystallizes in her nose and mouth.

Millie doesn't know how long they run until Fel stops and releases her hand. The sidhe bends and grasps one of the trees for support, sucking in deep breaths through her nose.

Millie sets a hand on Fel's shoulder. "Are you okay?"

"Yeah, that just took a lot out of me. Not the running or anything. The glamor."

"Yeah."

Instinctively, Millie massages her fingers into Fel's shoulders to warm her, ground her, or both. Whatever might help even a little bit.

"Sorry," Fel mutters.

Millie's mouth tightens. "No, don't be sorry." It just sort of pours out, bitingly curt. She should've said something that had more tact. Reassuring and simple. *It's okay.* Too late, already.

Stupidly, she pulls a pine needle from Fel's hair. It tingles with an essence only she can feel.

Not now.

She wishes that she could do something. She wishes that she was as powerful as Fel. That she knew more than how to create salves and potions because, sure, it's a great and potent power, but what good is it now? She *could* be powerful, if her witch soul would cooperate.

But she also knows the price.

Fel sucks a deep breath through her nose and straightens. "It's through here. We're close."

They continue up the hill at a slower pace, as Millie listens closely for rustling bushes and footsteps and sirens. Even the distant echoes of a dog's bark sends a shiver down her spine. But the only persistent sound is the murmur of rain.

As briars sting a slice of her cheek, Millie isn't sure how many lonely New England woods and roads they rush across until, through the slash of rain, they see glowing headlights and the familiar red of Simon's Ford Explorer.

Before they can approach the car, Millie's shocked when he actually gets out, her throat tight when he runs to them and, in a single fluid motion, throws his arms over Millie; even after their breakups, both Simon and Fel were always affectionate toward her.

Millie's always had a reputation as not-a-hugger, which made people think that she didn't like to be touched. Truth was that she's never known when someone wants to be hugged or touched, has never been good at reading the situation, so she avoids initiating anything.

Despite being cold and wet and ready to be under a roof, whether a car's or a house's, she breathlessly returns his strong hug, warm with the magic thrumming in his veins.

"Oh, thank God," Simon says, pulling away, brown eyes bright with genuine relief that makes Millie's heart skip.

In prison, it was so easy to imagine that everyone, even those who only treated her kindly, was laughing at her fate, if they even remembered her at all.

Her brain is truly her worst enemy.

She's relieved when they're in the car; she achingly stretches out in the back with a blanket over her entire body as rain patters the windows. But before she pulls the cotton over her head, she sees Simon as he is, just a little damper: a long brown ponytail streaked prematurely gray, and a dark blue jacket over a gray tunic that matches his pants and passes over the pouch of his belly; he always used to joke about being unable to have kids but having a dad bod.

She's missed both of them so much.

The rest of the night is quiet enough to make Millie suspicious.

Nevertheless, no one says much, and despite the tense moment, she hears Fel's deep snores in the passenger seat. The sound stirs her heart and memories of long, winter-bright mornings with Fel splayed across a mountain of pillows, legs tangled in the sheets. Fel used to tease Millie for being a much more considerate bed partner, since Millie often rolled on her side in one spot and stayed there the entire night. And she certainly never once darted out with the sheets dragging because she saw the shadow of a squirrel behind the curtains.

Millie sadly smiles.

The memories only grow as they reach their destination, and Millie is both relieved by its warm familiarity and apprehensive.

This is Fel's house. Maybe she and Simon share it now. Probably. Millie remembers the relief when she first moved in here, so far away from home down South. She hadn't used Fel as an escape, at least she didn't mean to, but she couldn't help but feel as if she had escaped.

And here you are again, escaping.

Just like that, her legs only just thawing from the cold with the cozily toasty car heat, Millie gets out, her feet hitting pavement, a familiar little crack where dandelions grow in the spring. She follows them up the little incline to the brick steps, and inside—

It's different. Changed. The grandfather clock near the dead fireplace isn't ticking anymore. But there's still that midnight-blue wallpaper with golden and green leaves twining from the ceiling to the deep gray carpet. The plush green recliners and, past the living room, the simple teal-tiled kitchen with small counter space. Even in the dim light of a nearby cheap standing lamp, she sees shards of obsidian and amethyst, for protection, next to a TARDIS figurine on the mantel; yeah, Simon has absolutely moved in.

We once shared this house. A bed.

After the escape, she's cold and hollowed out.

Millie learned that up in New England there are "witch houses" where people who believed in folk magic would put bottled bones behind the walls of their houses and especially around the chimney to ward off ghosts and malignant spirits; because the chimney is the open gullet of a house, it's the easiest place for entities to come through. Some people would even bury their dead pets behind the stones.

Of course, a lot of the mumbo jumbo about "evil forest spirits" was weird anti-indigenous sentiment, but it's true that everywhere in the world there are both good and bad entities from innumerable worlds with names Millie doesn't know. Most, like people, are just a mix of good and bad.

I'm safe here. Even Simon's wards say so. Focus on that.

If only her brain would retain that feeling. She's safe. Saved by the exes. That'd make a good book title.

Simon flicks his wrist at the fireplace, and flames spring to life, the wood crackling.

Millie crosses her arms over herself. Her mouth is dry. "I don't know how to repay you."

Simon whirls around and blinks at her. Both he and Fel do. Perfect. Millie can feel how she's being perceived. She doesn't want to be perceived; she wants to sleep. That's all. And tomorrow, she'll figure things out, starting with what those "things" will be.

He holds up his hands. "Damn, Mills." *Mills.* Like a knife. Why does kindness hurt more than hate? She can tell herself she doesn't care what her mom thinks of her anymore; she can't do that with Fel or Simon. "Maybe there can be reimbursement if, say, I pay five bucks for someone's meal one time. But getting you out of prison way too late? I don't want anything from you."

That's almost worse than if he, or Fel, demanded she give them a favor. Because now she's standing here, useless, unsure what to do with her hands with her nerves twitching like a hundred little fires under her skin.

So, aching and nervous and somehow numb all at once, Millie plops her butt down on the couch, right where that one cushion dips lower than the others.

Simon tells her, "I made up the guest room." Something about the sentence is a rejection, even though Millie knows she's being stupid. *Obviously, they aren't going to let you share the bed with them.*

Millie's jaw hardens as she squeezes her hands together and digs her fingers into the flesh near her knuckles. "I can't stay here." Logically, she has nowhere else to go, so she should. But the idea that Fel and Simon have done this much for her, and she could get them in trouble...

Fel says blearily, rubbing her eyes, "Yes, you can." She says it with the added, hard exhaustion of someone trying to douse an argument they expect.

Millie looks at the curtained window, watching for headlights. "If I'm found here, you'll be in a hell of a lot of trouble. It's too much of a risk."

Fel interjects, pacing and batting her own ear twice as if getting rid of a scratch, "If you go out there, you'll be in a hell of a lot of trouble!"

"At least I'll be taking the fall for what I did. That's different from taking you both down with me."

Simon gives a small nod, drawing in his bottom lip in thought, head bowed in what seems like resignation. Makes sense. They've been in these kinds of arguments before. Just, well, she hadn't been an escaped convict before; everything that bothered her before feels so trivial. "You aren't a serial killer, Mills. You're a hero."

There are killers who've gotten less than thirty years.

Millie hums. "I haven't saved anyone yet. And a conviction is a conviction." When she says it, she forgets momentarily which meaning of "conviction" she was going with at the start of the sentence.

There's a thrill to being a runaway prisoner, except for the dampening realization that she'll always have to keep her fugitive status in mind wherever she goes in case she's recognized and dragged back to prison.

Fel scratches the side of her head. "We can talk more later, but now, I think we should all get some sleep." Always to the point in that way Millie likes.

She's right. Guilt gnaws at Millie's gut for keeping Fel up. She tightened her arms over her chest. "You're right. I'm not going anywhere tonight, anyway."

She looks across the living room hall to see the shadows of another room, the workout room, where Fel always religiously went at six in the evening. Not today though.

I've missed them.

Simon tells Millie, "Here, I got some of your old clothes in the guest room, so you don't need to be in..." He stares at her prison uniform, which Millie can't quite feel on her body anymore. "That thing."

"Thanks. But maybe you should take a shower first. You look exhausted." Millie knows that Fel hates baths, the feeling of stewing in water.

"I know by the time you get out, the water will be hot again."

"Whoa, that's so true, but hardly called for."

"Besides, I spend some nights running around in fields and woods. The cold and wetness doesn't bother me." She gives a little tremble.

Millie hesitates. "If you're sure."

"Yeah, I'm sure." Fel awkwardly scratches her ear. "I'm not the one who, you know." Spent half a year in jail. Is that the new unspeakable thing?

Millie blinks some rain from her eyes. "It just doesn't feel real, I guess. Just a hazy, gray dream."

She feels bad complaining because her treatment in prison was dehumanizing because of the neglect and removal from the world; but she wasn't treated horribly by either the guards or the other prisoners. What she went through was nothing compared to the humiliation and horror that others go through. A correctional officer had once given her a glance over being saying, in what she thought was a compliment, "Oh, wow. you don't look like you belong here, like most of the others."

She thought about pulling the alarm. *I hope that I did the right thing. Maybe one day, I can do more.*

A lot of people have it worse in the justice system and prison, a place that now just exists for prisoners to be free, or very shittily paid, labor, and then told when they get out that, no, no jobs for you, no apartments for you, and no voting for you.

Community, what community? She remembers when a cousin got caught selling meth, and Mom would scold her for even saying his name. Millie didn't learn that she had an uncle until she was twenty-one because, after he was found shot and dead in an Atlanta alleyway, the family refused to speak about him.

And that was wrong. Being forgotten. Invisible.

Yet, saying, oh, don't worry about me, it wasn't that bad rings false, though. She needs more time to think about it. Process.

Pain flickers in Fel's eyes. "Yeah. I can't imagine, besides what I saw. I'm so sorry."

Millie shakes her head. "Look, it's...it's passed, right?"

Rubbing the back of his head, Simon offers a soft smile. "Yeah. We'll figure things out. We'll talk."

They love me, and I don't know what to do with it. I never know what to do with it.

First things first, Millie decides that she's taking a bath. A long one.

The guest bedroom she's staying in has deep blue wallpaper and sheets stippled with constellations. It's small with a closet and a writing desk, but it's perfect.

Another door leads to the bathroom, with another closet and a garden tub. A beautiful, beautiful garden tub. Millie doesn't hesitate to dump her uniform on the floor, kicking it into a little crumpled heap under the sink counter. She'll put it in the laundry basket once she's had a long bath.

And, God. It feels like forever since she's had a bath this nice. Or, well, just a regular steamy bath that didn't smell of that soap that gave her a rash and made her scalp itch.

And she's in a space where she can linger and daydream.

Her eyes burn when she sees the array of scents. Coconut and lavender—Simon. Citrus and pine—Fel. The achy muscles in her upper back lose a little tension, and she submerges herself in the steamy water until everything but her face is in the bleary hot limbo.

By the time she gets out of the cooled water, her fingers and toes are shriveled prunes, and she gives a laugh as she remembers being a little girl and making her fingers look like raisins. It wasn't until Mom disapprovingly commented on her wrinkled fingers that Millie started taking shorter baths.

Hair still a little damp, she enters the bedroom she's staying in. All her stuff is here, mostly neatly kept in the closet, but she can smell the pine laundry detergent of her recently re-washed clothes; they really did go to her apartment and make sure everything was safely kept. She puts on a loose gray shirt and her favorite pair of boxers, scarlet flannel.

On the desk sits a framed photo of her at her high school graduation with her grandma and grandpa. A lump forms in her throat.

I can't go home again. Because even if I did, it's not home anymore.

Millie's throat constricts as she tries to swallow the ball of phlegm. She needs to decompress. Rest. Not go down the rabbit hole of existential dread.

She lights the moon-yellow pumpkin spice and coconut candle on the desk and, after getting almost every pillow out of the closet, lies down on to a mountain of downy softness, taking a minute to suck air through her nose and release it out of her mouth. And damn it, these stupid exercises help. She lets the heavy top quilt mold over her body.

Need to blow out the candle.

That's the last thing she thinks before she shuts her eyes.

Chapter 3

Despite her usual luck, she doesn't wake up to the house on fire. The next morning, Millie wakes up, and instead of rain on concrete, stale sweat, mothballs, and potato vodka, fresh bold coffee spirals through the air, alongside the gentle song of fresh linens and a pine candle burning low on the writing desk across from the bed. Startled at her thoughtlessness, she rises and crosses the room to blow it out, the flame glancing near the bottom of the glass jar.

It takes her a few times, and she almost feels as if the flame is connected to her, tugging at that part of her heart where her witch soul stays.

You're losing it, Mills.

Eventually, she extinguishes the flame, waxy smoke in her nostrils, and she returns to the bed, as if it belongs to her. She adjusts to a sitting position, and her back pops, not quite adjusted to comfort. She lets it sink into the memory foam pillow and releases an easy sigh through her nose. She doesn't even remember going to bed, just getting out of the tub.

Nice.

That scares Millie, the comfort, because she expects, as the saying goes, for the other shoe to drop. She can never be content for long.

There's another smell: eggs and fresh biscuits.

For a moment, she closes her eyes and pretends that she hasn't spent the past six months in a cell.

To call prison "Hell" feels dramatic because most of the time, prison might've been soul-sucking, but it wasn't torture. There was no survival instinct or spite-driven teeth-gritting.

No. It was *boring*. But she had shelter and food. So, it feels stupid complaining about how unpersoned she felt there. Aimless. Exhausted and listless despite doing little, her brain fogged by a constant malaise. Eventually, she even grew used to shitting and showering with an audience.

It's done. It's over. Just enjoy the day.

Doing what?

The soft greens of the kitchen soothe Millie as she sits across from Simon and Fel at a table that looks more like a picnic bench.

She sits at an angle, so her right ear is facing both Simon and Fel as they chat about grocery store coupons and a sale on sirloin, Fel's favorite.

Millie has a more difficult time hearing out of her left ear than her right, but it's always felt strange calling herself hard of hearing or partially deaf, like she hasn't earned it because she hasn't gone to a doctor about it and hasn't gotten hearing aids since she's never been super inconvenienced.

She doesn't know her level of loss, only that anything out of her left ear is muffled; when she'd go to sleep with the TV on, she'd rest on her right side, so she achieved that perfect balance of having ambient noise without focusing too hard on what people were saying, since she could barely make them out. It never feels like a huge burden, except when her tinnitus goes *woosh woosh woosh,* which almost drove her off the deep end in her cell.

Is it a disability if it sometimes has a benefit? If it's something she doesn't mind having when her peers at college would treat it like a Big Deal and a huge secret she hid from them to try to cheat them out of feeling good for sitting on the right side to help out a disabled person?

Maybe. She's not sure. It took her a year into dating Fel before she even casually mentioned her hearing loss. There was no great reason she had her disability; when she was a kid, it was always there. Is it a disability if her lack of good left-hearing inconveniences other people (Millie: "Sorry, can you say that again?" Mom: "Ugh, Emelia, stop being lazy and listen for once.") more than it does her?

As she eats, Millie slathers hot sauce on her scrambled eggs, and her mouth bursts with flavor as she stuffs her face. The best biscuits she's ever had were her granny's homemade ones, but these ones are pretty great, so soft and buttery that they almost melt in her mouth. God. She could get used to this.

Again, the idea frightens her.

There was a time when she thought she'd never be caught, that she'd be fine just getting by.

"How is it?" Simon asks. Yeah, Millie can be blunt, but like she'll ever say, oh, it sucks.

"Mm. This is great. My stomach is going to have to adjust to eating this."

Fel levels her a hooded gaze. "Is the food, you know, *there* really as bad as it is in movies?"

"Sometimes, it's fine. Depends. The eggs were always made from powder, but with hot sauce, they were bearable."

The topic passes.

What makes the ongoing day worse is not that anything goes wrong.

Not that there's some huge, cataclysmic argument. Millie almost wishes there was some sort of drama to justify her need to leave.

It's only that she realizes increasingly that she's not sure what to say to Fel or Simon. After being in prison for half a year, she knows that if she talked about it, they'd listen, but she's not exactly sure what to bring up or if they'd understand.

The day passes, and Millie sits around, cards her fingers through different books, from herbology to fiction, and finds that she has no interest in reading anything. Writing? No. If it were warmer, she might garden. Simon has a cauldron downstairs and an assortment of herbs, crystals, animal bones, gems, and so on, but she can't think of what she could make.

In the end, she sits at the end of the guest bed and contemplates everything she doesn't feel like doing with a calm detachedness. She looks in the closet to find an old traveling bag of hers, complete with expired granola bars and bottles of water she kept in it. Truly, Simon and Fel kept everything as close to as it was as they could.

A lump forms in her throat, and she plans.

Another day passes, and evening comes. She watches an old sitcom with Simon and Fel; normally, she doesn't like comedies, but it's nice in a way that a horror movie might not be.

I can't drag them down with me. I have to go. Go where? I don't know. Just go. It's a dick move in the short-term and a mercy in the long-term.

But she doesn't want them to worry. A naïve thought. Obviously, they'll worry no matter what.

Millie hates that she's lonely, but she hates even more when Simon and Fel try to be close to her.

Because it didn't work out. Because both her exes probably cuddle in bed and think of all the ways she failed both of them by being paradoxically too clingy and too aloof. Maybe they even laugh about her intimacy issues and the first time she cried during sex. Why shouldn't they?

She's a mess, and they know. They know, they saw, and she can't take that back. They know too much because she gave them too much and too little. They know about her family's rejection, her drive to do good and fuck the rules and what The Man says is right, i.e. legal.

I've dragged them into crime with me.

That witch soul inside her croons, *They chose that. Would you take their decision from them, so you can martyr yourself? Poor, tormented little witch. Everyone rejects you, so might as well run.*

Millie ruffles. "Fuck you. I'm not doing it because you told me to."

Whatever you say, Mills. Believe it or not, but I don't want you to get hurt either.

I won't get hurt, Millie thinks, the door knob cool. No tickling on her palm, no charms; Simon really trusts her, huh. But why did she assume he'd try to set an alarm or trap her, when he's never done that before? *I know how to take care of myself.*

"Sorry," Millie mutters, shutting the door behind her. It sounds louder than it is, ricocheting in the dusty halls of her mind, which all look like a prison.

All I have is myself.

All I deserve is myself.

Chapter 4

This is a mistake. No matter what you do or say, they'll worry. You have no money, no other clothes, no cell phone. If you run into the police—or a gaunt—you're fucked.

Millie shuts her eyes and forces herself to take a deep breath, letting the winter air bite her lungs.

All relationships are water. Everyone leaves, and it's better to be the one who leaves first.

Better to be solitary.

Better to be alone.

Less risk.

She'll fuck up others less this way. If she's ruined her own life this badly, she'll surely do it to Simon and Fel. This is for the best. It's fine.

A shock of goosebumps spreads across her body as the world seeps through. She keeps checking her left side.

No gaunts yet.

Rustling to her right. Millie hurries faster, as a squirrel darts out of a bush and rushes up a tree. Between lowered vein-fingers of leafless branches, street lamps burn like blurry full moons in the thick fog. One twitches with a darting black spot: a trapped moth frantically trying to escape.

Already feeling that hitch in her chest, Millie stops and shuts her eyes, trying to let her mind-fingers touch the warmth in the center of her chest, which has always been more tepid than blazing like she's been told witch souls are supposed to be

She imagined the glass melting. Disappearing from reality.

When she opens her eyes, nothing has changed, except that something about the moth feels more frenzied.

"Sorry, little guy," Millie mutters to herself as she keeps walking. "I tried."

As she moves on, she keeps checking her left side for any disturbances.

This isn't selfish. This isn't selfish. This isn't selfish. I'm a fugitive. I have a demon in me. I'm saving them.

She still hasn't gotten used to how bone-cold New England can be; she just liked the idea of a storied place like Massachusetts, with towns like Salem. And then, close by, Rhode Island and the sea. Down home in Ellijay, she couldn't just drive or take a cab or bus to see the ocean.

Somehow, it felt more romantic than the little Appalachian towns filled with Bigfoot festivals—poor Bigfoot; as far as fae creatures go, Mothman appreciates the attention much more—and blood-red political signs that stay up years after major presidential elections, and it all made her feel stuck. Stuck with people who hate her, who don't respect her humanity and then chastise her for not respecting their opinions. Stuck in time. Stuck pretending and being worn down. Stuck in survival mode and hypervigilance every second of the day, even when she was asleep, or trying to sleep.

She can't tell if it's the surrounding darkness that's dampening her mood and dragging her into melancholy. It's a different sort of night from Southern country darkness amid the red clay and wild blackberry patches that became her haunts.

The air smells wet with dew and a tang of salt; she's close to the ocean, but she can't hear it.

She finds herself in a town, but not the one she and Fel would usually go into. This one looks almost deserted. A ghost town surrounded by woods. Sounds about right. She treads warily on a street where the shops are closed beneath their striped awnings, the asphalt slicked with muddy rain puddles.

A mossy, faded, water-streaked sign under a shuddering street lamp reads, *Forgotten Hill, 1591.*

Ah. Yeah. How very New England gothic.

She's heard of this town before, but not much outside of it being mentioned as a place to pass through on the way to Arkham or Boston. Coastal town, population probably below a thousand. Has a vampire lord who keeps to himself with his domain being his manor—more of a castle—on a hill.

Only the lights from the streetlamps and a nearby building strike the asphalt and puddles. Millie steps closer to the one building with a warm orange glow. An old-timey tavern, or what Millie guesses a New England tavern in Old-Timey would look like a place in a game where you'd pick up quests. An angular, clean arrangement of gray stones below wooden planks and a red gable roof that reaches a point in two places, like horns. The stone steps and ramp are also gray, in contrast with the brown beams and...are those *torches* burning in the dead of night?

Smart. Gaunts don't like fire, though she's unsure if a ravenous one would be deterred by such small flames.

The windows, despite their stern iron latticing, are round in a way that makes the tavern gentler to her, as silly as it sounds. She can't say, however, that she's heartened by the box of dead flowers.

Approaching the window, while trying to not directly stand in the light, Millie pinches one of the wilted brown stems. No, not even a trace of Azoth left.

She shuts her eyes, waits, and huffs. Her grandma could make roses come back to life with a single touch, her witch soul reaching out and interacting with the Azoth.

Millie opens her eyes to look to the right.

In spiky script, a hanging sign reads, *The Wilted Carnation.* No false advertising, at least.

She steps back and hesitates. Smoke curls lazily out of the chimney. Mm, warmth. She rubs her chilled fingers together. Shouldn't have forgotten gloves. Stupid. Maybe there's still time to head back.

The soft murmur of inside conversations rolls over her like cicadas in summer.

What's the worst that can happen if she goes inside the tavern? Well, someone in this little town recognizes her, and she gets arrested again. While she definitely doesn't want to go back to prison, she can't say that she's as afraid as she thought she'd be. She knows what it's like to be in prison, so it feels less scary. That, or it's the numbness, like the brain fog after a panic attack, that blunts her worry. It's not exactly a lack of self-preservation, but nevertheless, it makes her more reckless.

When she opens the swinging door, and a little bell rings, she squints when the amber lights beam into her eyes.

She's struck by the miasma of Old Spice, Axe body spray, and sweat that pools into her nostrils and stings. But also, the lingering scents of fresh bread and beer. A haven in the gloom. A haven with dead flowers, but Millie knows that death is everywhere, has seen the life-blood drain from so many things, even herself, almost, when a gaunt attacked her, and the police found her with her lower face completely mottled by blood.

I'm safe. It's warm.

I'm safe.

She knows it isn't true, and she's not sure when it'll be true again.

She wants to tell herself that she's so far from the prison, and that it isn't like anyone is as worried about an illegal gaunt cure-maker fleeing as they would be if she were a worse criminal. And there are other things, too. Even with a thirty-year sentence, she's fortunate to have the ability to fade into the background. A lot of people don't have that and come under instant scrutiny just for existing. The guys here, about six in the booths near the fireplace, barely glance at her.

Still, her stomach is a tight knot. She's gone from the same routine day after day to not knowing where she'll be in the next hour.

So much for the nationwide curfew. Good luck enforcing it. Even in the face of roaming bat monsters and death counts in the four digits, some wouldn't dare let the presence of infernal creatures impede on their freedoms to go outside in the middle of the night and get eaten.

She hopes that the food and drinks here are really that good, but despite the faintness in her head, she can't bring herself to order anything. She just needs to sit. Sit and think, away from people that she knows that she'll eventually disappoint. That's why she sometimes liked talking to strangers better than good acquaintances; strangers never expect much from her.

Despite her worries, a thrill goes through her. She has drive, a purpose; she's always acted when there's danger, an inch from a gaunt snapping its sword-teeth, and despite her fatigue, she got afraid at the thought of living *without* peril. Her time with Fel and Simon had been nice, but she always had too much awareness of herself and her shortcomings without some external problem forcing her to act in survival mode.

Behind the lacquered counter, a man with a deep brown apron and thinning dark blonde hair booms to her, "Hello! Welcome! Please make yourself at home." His belly is a soft pouch under the apron, and there are dark circles under his brown eyes. A heater churns in the corner, a false fire flickering in the square black box.

Millie gives a perfunctory smile and nods. "All right, thanks." A year ago, she could never have predicted those words would come out of her mouth, even if gaunts have apparently been around for a while. Most just hid in mountains and forests and became legends.

The bartender explains, "We ain't Boston, but the cabs run all night, and they have silver in them, so you should be safe if any of those things show up." Millie is sure every car has silver in it. "They don't get attacked. Usually."

"Okay," Millie replies, unrelieved. "I'll keep that in mind, thanks."

Being safe inside a cab would require having money and getting inside the vehicle without getting eaten. Lots of variables. She was surprised there was a closing time at all, given how many business owners, from small mountain towns in the South where she lived to historical places like Salem, Massachusetts, clamored about the curfew because they'd lose business from tourists. "I just, I just need a moment to compose myself."

He nods, brow scrunched in sympathy. Pity. Great. "All right. Just let me know if you need anything. I'm Brian."

"Great, thanks, Brian." She should've been courteous and given her name, but it's not safe, and her throat is dry and swollen and feels like she's a second away from hacking out a lung.

Hiding her shivering hands in her sleeves, Millie finds an unoccupied corner booth, behind three men talking about how this winter is supposed to be the coldest one in hundreds of years. Colder, and darker, and they wonder if that means the bat-monster attacks will get worse. Millie slumps down in the green booth with a single rip in the middle of the seat. Leaning, she crosses her arms on the table.

A burgeoning pain pierces her cranium; great, what she needs right now is a migraine. she only hopes it doesn't turn out like the ones in college that'd make her lie in bed all day and vomit.

One of the men in the booth next to hers says to his companions, "I wonder if that vampire'll show up tonight."

Curious, Millie raises her voice and asks, "What vampire?" So much for discretion, but she can't help herself.

One of the men, a man who looks like he's forty-something with salt-and-pepper hair, leans and tells her, "There's this man and woman who live with the vampire lord on top of Forgotten Hill. The woman will bring stories to the kids, and the man brings blankets and clothes."

Many regions have a vampire lord; big cities tend to have more than a handful with their own claimed domains. Feeding grounds, certain news outlets would proclaim, but it's more complicated than that, especially when most vampires drink from blood bags instead of people. They have land and properties that they own, but mostly, they act as mentors and guardians for others like them, which aren't a huge number.

And then there's Forgotten Hill with a vampire who apparently keeps to himself. Or three vampires? She remembered that there was at least one, and she can almost see his face from a local newspaper stand she passed, talking about a donation to the local library.

She inquires further, "Are both the man and woman who live with the lord vampires, too?"

"Yeah. I was talking about the man—the other one, the blonde one, not the one that looks like a villain in one of those games, you know, the Konami ones." Millie doesn't know. *Silent Hill?* Does Konami still make games? "Silver hair. Wasn't too sure about the blonde one at first, the other guy, because of, well, his mannerisms, but he does good things."

"Oh," Millie replies, "I see. Cool. Thanks for letting me know." *His mannerisms.* She almost wants to come to the defense of a stranger. She doesn't know what the "mannerisms" are, but by the way the man's voice drew out the word, she has an idea.

She racks her brain with her memories of researching what vampire lords she knows.

Most vampires are clandestine about their pasts, while others, such as the Baroness Claudia Tremblay, have written bestselling memoirs about being forced to marry at fourteen and, in her early adulthood, living through the French Revolution, leading to a burst of historians feuding over whether she *really* talked to the likes of Marie Antoinette and the Marquis de Sade, whether she *really* slept with Louis Antoine de Saint-Just on the golden altar of Sacre-Coeur Basilica at the crown of the Mount of Martyrs, and whether the unfortunate Baron Tremblay was *really* guillotined before Claudia fled the fate of her fellow Girondins.

But the vampire lord of Forgotten Hill, she can't quite remember much about him. *It's Matthew, Matthew Something.* No, that wasn't right; Matthew wasn't a very vampire-y name, but then again, if you get bitten and changed and your name is Earl, then technically, Earl must be a vampire name.

The entrance door swings open, and Millie tenses, as if expecting a gaunt to casually lumber through the front entrance. Instead, the person who glides in is a man that must be around her age—or he was in his first life.

With ease, the man approaches the bar. In the crook of his arm, he carries a weighed down white tote bag with golden flowers stitched into it. His blue coat, a more robust shade than his dark trousers, is lined with gold flower patterns, and his gloves are as white as his tunic with the ruffled front that looks like something out of a historical reenactment.

Flowing locks of golden—her mind goes to "flaxen"—hair furl down his shoulders, and black eyeliner rings his blue cat-eyes.

Unmistakably, wickedly beautiful, and unmistakably a vampire. Millie would say it's this air of sumptuous decadence with an air of haughtiness, or the ethereality, but really, it's the pointed ears.

Despite trying to keep a low profile, Millie can't stop staring at him. It's probably the damned eyeliner; Simon sometimes wears it, and she can't turn down a guy with good eyeliner. Mom never understood, scoffing and rolling her eyes. *I could never date a sissy.*

That's fine, Millie replied, knowing a fight was what her mother wanted if she took the bait and protested. *More for me.*

She can't say that she's never been curious about being with a vampire. The idea scares her, which only entices her more. Hell, she's been with another witch and a wolf-fae, hasn't she?

It's been about six years that vampires, at least, have been out in the open—out of the coffin, so to speak, and it's been about the same time that many began losing themselves at faster rates than expected.

And on one hand, besides the gaunt attacks that make most people stay inside at night, not much has changed, since the world is still a dumpster fire; on the other hand, the amount of news coverage about supernatural beings skyrocketed, and so did the conspiracy theories.

And Millie, well. Fae, witches, vampires, they were all people with different needs.

She could say with utmost certainty though that, on an aesthetic level, she wouldn't say no to this guy; he was definitely one of her types, in the way that she admired a textbook print of a John Keats portrait in college. Those soft, distant eyes and long curls.

This vampire, though, has something sharp about him. Makes sense. Even John Keats got into scuffles, amputated limbs in doctor school, and wrote about a lady lovingly keeping a decapitated head in a basil pot.

The blonde vampire sets a wooden box on the counter. It's stunning, as far as boxes go. Dappled with pink and red roses on top and with a metal lock in the front. Looking closer, she also sees the faint imprints of gray wolves running between the petals.

Then, the undead man speaks, "Hello, Brian, how are you, and how is your family?" His voice is silken but quick, with a French accent; Millie is surprised at first, but she guesses that she shouldn't be. Most of the well-known vampires come from the Old World. Hell, the infamous Claudia Tremblay is French. She can't say that it's a surprise. Who wouldn't want to get turned in Paris, a city looming over a labyrinth of bones?

Brian says, scratching a pink rash on the back of his neck, "We're all doing all right, Mr. Laflamme. Er, Monsieur."

Monsieur Laflamme waves a friendly hand.

Some calendula and lavender petals would do Brian good. Despite not knowing where she'll be in the morning, Millie makes a note that if she ever sees Brian again, she'll give him the ingredients for a nice rash-relieving bath, which she learned when she played as a kid and plummeted into a lovely tangle of poison ivy.

A bright grin that lights up the vampire's entire face. "Wonderful. I have what you asked for."

Millie can only stare in curiosity as the stylish vampire takes a key from the bag and unlocks the box, opening it to reveal an array of pretty pastel knitted—socks? Booties, like for a baby. Pink, orange, green, blue. The image confuses her. That's not exactly something she expects a vampire to be carrying around after midnight. Or any time.

Brian raises one of the little green booties, his eyes bright. "Thank you so much. You know, little Lyddie, she gets colder than the rest. She shakes, no matter what we do."

The vampire smiles gently. "Hopefully, that stops that. She's very beautiful, you know, especially that wavy hair."

Brian's voice catches, like he's about to cry. "Thank you."

Millie remembers what the other guests said about the vampire; after all, it was three minutes ago. But she guesses she didn't expect this particular elegant, dramatic, sexy—*damn it,* but she has eyes—vampire to be the one carrying around clothes for little babies who get cold. That doesn't exactly get written about, not as much as the illicit affairs and soul-corrupting murders, but why wouldn't someone use their eternal time and skills to do nice, little things? She's captivated—

The vampire looks right in the corner at her, and he holds her stare for a second, before looking back at Brian and entering a casual conversation. The entire air of the warm tavern has shifted, and she thinks that everything has settled, all except for the compelling and animated vampire speaking to Brian. Monsieur Laflamme, who she cannot help but find beautiful.

Millie tenses in wariness, looking down at her crossed arms, which ache, as do her tired eyelids. If only she could curl up in this booth and sleep.

She can't trust anyone now.

A voice enters her head.

May I?

Straightening in shock, she looks up to see the vampire with both hands in his trouser pockets, standing at a distance. Everyone else in the tavern have resumed their conversations and laughter, the air smelling of woodsmoke, warm bread, and beer. Her belly grumbles.

Guess Monsieur Laflamme is a regular.

Despite her surprise, she meets his eyes unflinchingly. If her resolve annoys him, he doesn't show it. His eyes glint with an emotion she can't discern.

She thinks to him, *You're already here. You won't read my mind, will you?*

Nothing, except what you project to me.

Okay, then help yourself.

With the fluidity of dogwood petals in an autumn gust, Monsieur Laflamme sits across from her. He regards her with an inquisitive brow lifted in amusement, a finger set upon the pink bow of his lips.

Forgive me if the observation is insensitive, but you look absolutely worn.

Spare me. What do you want, blondie?

Ah, I was hoping for some banter tonight.

Great. Glad to please.

I'll cut to the chase. I recognize you, Emelia Byron.

Chapter 5

Millie starts, slapping her hands against the table. Slowly, as if showing his goodwill, the vampire takes off both his gloves. He holds up his own fingers, circled with rings, including two bands, one gold, one black, with his nails painted mauve. It's pretty, but doesn't quite fit with his outfit.

It's okay, the vampire tells her. *Relax.* Easy for him to say! *I'm not going to turn you in. What sort of company would I have if I turned in everyone I know who's done a crime? Hell, I'd have to turn myself in, too.*

Are you going to blackmail me?

No. Don't insult me like that. I don't think you did anything wrong, but I didn't expect to see you milling about, no pun intended.

What do you want?

From you? Nothing. Though I'm curious how you were released so early.

Can't you tell? Good behavior.

But we both know you've escaped. Good for you.

Thanks, Millie replies, not quite as tense.

What are your plans, exactly?

Don't get caught.

A sensible plan, Emelia, if abstract. We can't always control what others do, such as if they choose to catch us.

Call me Millie. Not Emelia. I don't like that name.

Her mom would call her it even when she asked for her not to, insisting that it was actually the utmost respect to call her a name that she hated because, in the end, she was reminding Millie of who she *really* is. Or, more to the point, who she's *supposed* to be. That, or pulling the *You're the one disrespecting me by not liking that name—me, your mother, the one who gave birth to you, in case you forgot* card.

Emelia: Good. Respectable. Christian. Straight.

Millie: Queer, slutty fuck up embarrassment and escaped convict.

She still likes "Millie" better. Besides, her most powerful ancestor wanted to fuck a fallen angel and succeeded. She feels like she's a lot more in line with family tradition than most of her close blood relatives.

I see, Millie. If you want, you can come home with me. At the very least, so you may stay in one of the guest bedrooms and rest well.

Sorry, I tend to like to get a coffee before I go home with anyone. Etiquette and all.

Of course. I would be remiss if I were to offer you shelter but not a cup of whatever you like.

The vampire raises a curled hand and looks behind the booth at the counter. "Brian?"

Brian comes over. "Yeah, what do you need?"

"Do you have any coffee?"

"Not usually at this hour, but I can make some fresh," the man tells them.

The vampire gives a smile that makes her heart skip. Damn heart.

"When is there a better time? Anyone awake at that time must surely need some to remain so. In for a penny and all that, as the Brits say." He looks at her. "Are you hungry?"

Pivoting slightly to let her right side face the vampire, her hip seizing like it often does at night, Millie crosses her arms over herself. "Yeah. You paying?" Brusque, but it gets the job done.

"Naturally."

Do fancy vampires even get charged? You sound like a bit of a celebrity here.

He smirks. *Fancy vampires don't tend to buy meals at taverns.*

Touché, as the French say.

After she reads the menu behind the napkin holder, Millie orders a plate of cheese-stuffed shrimp jalapeño poppers and some honey BBQ hot wings. So, she ends up with a massive steaming plate and hot coffee, and her mouth waters. The world, even the vampire, fades, and she relishes the flavor of her food. The fullness once she's finished helps, and the coffee both gives her a buzz and soothes her.

She expected the vampire to smarmily press her on what to eat. She's had boyfriends do that before. And girlfriends. *Ew. You use too much salt; you've maxed out your sodium intake. Oh God, lay off the sweets. Your doctor won't take your chronic pain seriously at this weight.*

Not that he's her partner.

But also, not that she'd turn him down if he wanted to get down. A tug below her navel. What? She has eyes, and she has needs.

First things first.

"I hope that it was to your liking." She searches his tone for any sarcasm, but she finds nothing. "Do you have anywhere to go?"

"No. I escaped, and that's it. I have nowhere to go." A tug behind her eyes, which sting. Damn it.

"Come, you can stay where I live. There's certainly enough room. And you can be left well alone, if you want."

Millie straightens, instantly suspicious. "Why?"

"Because you need it." He makes it sound so simple. A good deed, like making little booties for little kids. Does this make her a charity case? Should she refuse just to spare what pride she has left?

Millie starts warily, "If they come after me..."

"Law enforcement?" asks the vampire.

"Yeah."

"I'm sure there's some enchantment that would make your appearance different. A glamor, that's what it is, isn't it?"

Millie gives a stiff nod. If only.

She can't admit that she's barely a witch without a cauldron and a room full of dried herbs and various jars of animal bones and candles. As much as the idea of knowing how to immolate something sounds appealing, she needs her mortar and pestle, and she finds a certain calm in getting lost in her work.

Yet, she wishes that she could at least pull off a glamor.

"Who are you living with?" Millie asks him. "I wouldn't want to disturb them."

"My two dearest companions."

Millie scratches the side of her head. "Right. I think I heard about that. You know, I'm not really, er, I'm not used to...I mean, prison had a lot of other people around all the time, but..."

Her eyes drift. Some of the others in the tavern is taking glances at them, some lingering more than others.

"I understand why you'd hesitate," he tells her, setting both arms on the table. She snaps her attention back to him. Surely, it hasn't escaped his notice that she's distracted. And sleepy. "Certainly, most mortals are cautious around one vampire, much less three. However, we are very careful about our needs."

"I recognize...Count Matthias Kos..."

"Matthias Kosztolányi."

"Matthias Kosztolányi," she repeats. "What is he like?"

The look that passes over the vampire's eyes is hard to describe in one word. Dreamy, maybe, accompanied by a softening of his features, which, since she's met him, have always been shrewd and alert, sharp as his cheekbones.

"He's a serious man. Attentive. Considerate."

"What about the woman? One of the guys in the tavern mentioned her."

His eyes glow with gentle affection. "Claire. Yes, she's my wife."

Claire. The name reminds her of a dessert. Or a bell, like the ones she'd hear on dewy Easter mornings before the church egg hunts. She likes it.

Unable to stop her curiosity, Millie inquires, "Did you all know each other before you were vampires?"

"I knew Claire; we were already married and living in Paris after the first World War. We were both still recovering from our past wounds, some more recent than others." Millie doesn't press him, though she's interested to learn more. "We met Matthias when he was already a vampire, and he changed us."

"Oh. Has he been around long? Is he powerful?"

"Yes."

Millie isn't sure how she feels about that. Part of her thinks that it'd be pretty cool to have a powerful vampire by her side. Three vampires sounds even better.

But if she can't even let Fel or Simon fully into her life, can she trust three strangers who can do much more than her?

Claire. Matthias. Millie realizes that she knows his partners' names before she knows his. "What's your name?"

"My name is Léon." It's a nice name. Feels warm, for some reason. She thinks of the sun.

He's so freely offering this information without digging any more about her. It makes her suspicious, and she hates that it does; the more he tries to respect her distance, these walls and locked doors, the more she wonders if it's some elaborate manipulation. Whether he'll lead her to handcuffs and a cell.

"Cool," is all Millie tells him, wincing at her own awkwardness. While she meets his steady gaze unflinchingly, it makes her weary; she used to avoid eye contact all the time, and it never fails to make her tired. Perceiving someone else perceiving her.

She sees herself, her drooping eyelids and deep frown, in his eyes.

"I feel like I'm always going to have to watch my back," Millie says, not quite sure why she's admitting it to him.

"You're a witch, aren't you?" It's a funny thing to ask, this thing they both know, but hell, *is* she? She ruffles. "As I said, perhaps you could conjure a glamor to keep others from seeing your true face."

"I can try." The idea of making a magical mask for herself has always been appealing, the idea of shielding yourself from being perceived. Millie shrugs. "I'm not that powerful. I can barely use a cauldron without it blowing up in my face."

"Not that powerful of a witch *yet*. Most aren't at your age."

"I'm almost thirty."

"Thirty, my God! You're halfway to the grave."

That makes her laugh. "Ooh, sarcasm, haven't heard that before."

"My dear, you make it sound like you're a wizened crone."

"I guess sometimes the back pain makes me feel like it." And the bouts of brain fog. Millie pauses. "What do you want?"

Léon regards her seriously. "I don't want anything from you. I'll leave you be, if that's what you need, but something tells me that you need help. I won't impose it on you if you want to be left alone, but I thought I'd try, if you wanted someone to listen. I have too many resources at my disposal to simply look the other way."

Listen? Listen to what? He knows everything. She's an escaped felon. She's a witch. Everything else feels insignificant. She should tell him to leave because this is her struggle, and no one else's responsibility.

A tug on her heart.

"Yeah. Please stay."

He does.

Millie racks her brains on her studies of vampires while she was trying to brew a cure for the gaunts. While she's not a huge vampire expert, she knows that things like the pointy ears mean Léon's killed at least a few people; the more people a vampire kills, the more their body changes from what they looked like in their mortal life. Unless his ears were always pointy, like Fel's, which Millie doubts.

Granted, she'd be damned if she said she didn't find the elfin ears to be pretty cool and sexy; she wasn't immune to a bi awakening from seeing Cate Blanchett with a shiny circlet and prosthetic elf ears.

And if the neat ears mean Léon has killed before, Millie couldn't even say that she's opposed to killing people, if the reason's right. It might sound bad, but she feels like her reasons for killing someone are pretty select. Would she lose sleep at night if someone murdered a person in self-defense, or killed somebody who'd been abusing and hurting them for years? Not really. When you have no other recourse, and no one will listen and step in for you, you have to do what you have to do.

She isn't sure how to escalate from "what are you companions' names" to "hey, so how many people have you killed and why?"

I want him to stay anyway. Is that so wrong?

This isn't a bad time. Any other moment, she'd love to sit across from a beautiful man and eat a full, indulgent meal and a hot cup of coffee. Maybe one day she can look back and think about this moment fondly, but she's been in survival mode for a long time. Taking everything day by day, hour by hour

Millie gets another cup of hot coffee despite knowing that it might make her hands shake more than they already were.

Unfortunately, as a pinch of her wariness subsides, she becomes more aware of some of the other conversations in the room. Most of the conversations are fine, but the hairs on her nape rise. She feels herself being watched from across the tavern.

A man is saying, his eyes flickering toward her, "She's a little on the chunky side, but I bet if she went to the gym, she'd be a good lay. I wonder what that fag wants with her. Why is it that all the pretty girls are attracted to sissies nowadays?"

The other man across from him waves a hand over a glass of pale beer. "Stop. You're being rude."

"I only call it like I see it."

She meets Léon's eyes, and she lets him in.

Would you like me to humiliate him? he asks her.

Nothing fatal, right?

The look that passes on Léon's face is a mix of horror and amusement. *I can't blame you for being wary, but no. Of course not.*

Make him piss himself. It's a nasty thought. Gross. Petty. She's sure Léon will say no. Admonish her for such a horrible thought. Léon continues to meet her eyes when there's a commotion in that one booth.

"I...God. God." The man stumbles to his feet, a dark stain blossoming on his jeans. His friend also stands, but the man is running out the door.

At the bar, Brian gives Léon an unamused glance and a raised brow, as if asking, *Did you really have to do that? Again?*

"I'll be sure to clean it," is all Léon says, twisting a finger around a curl. "I mean it."

Millie stares down at her own hands. *How much control do you have over humans? Complete control?*

Yes. I don't use it often.

That hint of darkness. The potential for meanness. Cruelty. It makes her trust him more. It means that he's at least a little like her. That maybe one time, not too long ago, he was lost and tired and angry, and the world told him to be good and roll over, and he said, *Fuck you.*

Another laugh bubbles up from deep in her chest.

Léon adjusts one of his jacket cuffs. "I'm quite used to comments like that."

Millie blurts, "I'm sorry."

"Don't be. I'm quite happy. The small-minded hurt themselves. And, naturally, sometimes we can help that process along."

They hurt themselves. It's a nice thought. True, that people who close themselves off to new experiences because they don't like a group of people diminish themselves. But a lot of them try to force their way of life on everyone else, and in the end, the people they target are the worst off.

Millie says, "I wish they *only* hurt themselves."

"Yes, but I can defend myself. I'll use that where I can, even if others think it's a little mean-spirited."

"So can I. But, you know, I still appreciate it. I think I like you."

"It's incredibly hard not to."

"Modest."

"After so long, you realize modesty doesn't do much good."

Something's wrong.

She first notices a tremor in her seafoam-green coffee cup, ripples in the dark roast.

Then, the building trembles. With inhuman speed, Léon stands and raises his voices to the rest of the tavern: "Everyone, get to the cellar! *Hide.*"

A chill creeps down Millie's spine, and she goes to stand, hastily slinging the travel bag over her shoulder.

A clamor of panicked footsteps to the back of the tavern. Brian ducks under the counter, but not before grabbing something under it—a rifle. Millie feels like she's back home again, where everyone from her mom to the ninety-year-old grandma living at the end of the street just...had stockpiles of guns.

Léon waves both hands in hard exasperation. "No, listen to me. Think of your daughters. Don't fight it, go!" His eyes then fall on Millie, but her feet are frozen.

Brian's Adam's apple bobs, his eyes wide with adrenaline and fear.

When the creature breaks down the tavern doors, its fur a chestnut brown, streaked with silver, its face is that of a long-eared bat. Its eyes, though, remind Millie of a lapis lazuli charged with a little magic, glittering globes of toxic blue.

The gaunt is a smaller one, but when it tries to fit into the door, it splits the frame and part of the wall as it bursts in. Millie sticks to the wall as it settles in the middle of the tavern, launching its sharply clawed feet on the bar with a scrape, its wings knocking into multiple bottles, which shatter into clouds of glass shards.

She loses Léon as she focuses on the gaunt, but she heard his words. Nevertheless, with the monster already in the room, she doesn't want to draw attention to the cellar where others are hiding.

The bat raises its long ears and its pear-shaped nose and sniffs the air. The tops of its wings are daggered with hand-like, knived claws.

Despite her magic being locked away, despite not knowing or understanding her own body or soul most of the time, she jolts her hand forward, and a streak of blue like spirals across the space and hits one of its wings, the webbed skin sizzling.

The gaunt howls and swivels its attention to her. She backs away, boots crunching on glass and wood splinters. She stumbles as a white flash of pain rakes down her left arm, but before it can bite a chunk out of her, it screeches and turns, and someone rushes past and grabs her left hand.

She runs with Léon, whose mouth is dripping with blood. They run out of the tavern, into the street, into the woods. Briars tug at her coat.

He *bit* the bat monster to distract it, which only seems to irritate it more, but what more can he do? What can *she* do? She's never known a gaunt to just attack the inside of a building before.

Maybe Léon's plan, in the end, is to distract the creature from everyone else, including her, maybe on sheer instinct, but she doesn't want him to die. She grabs for his hand while the gaunt shifts its massive body

"Can you turn into a bat?" Millie asks quickly, frantically making wing motions with her right hand. She's heard of vampires that can even turn into gaunts and still maintain control, but those vampires are very old and once committed great crimes.

Léon spits out light brown hair. "I can, but you cannot, which presents an issue of transportation. Unless you can. I unfortunately don't know many witches."

"I can't."

"Ah. Glad we cleared that up. There's a silver mine just down here..."

Millie struggles to reply, already breathless. Her run slows. Months and prison and two bouts of COVID make her lungs squeeze into a hard knot even more than her escape with Fel. Then, it was like a fire burst into her after so long.

Now... "Are—aren't you, you hurt by silver?" She swallows painfully. Her ankles throb.

"Not quite as much, so long as there's no touching any stray nodes." Léon gestures to her with both hands. "Trust me," he says hastily, looking behind her where the gaunt barrels toward them, crashing into trees and briars, slipping past them as if slicing through water.

And then it lunges, and spreads its wings, and a shadow falls over her.

Trust me.

A tall order.

I don't trust my closest friends. I don't trust my witch soul. I don't trust myself.

We have to jump.

Fuck it.

All of this in under a second.

Sucking in her pride, Millie gestures for Léon to come on already. He bends and dips his arms under her knees and behind her back, molding his palm and fingers fluidly to her sleeve. She has to keep from holding in her breath when her feet lift off the ground.

As Léon holds her bridal style, his boots careen to the edge of the dark chasm. Her heart lurches in her throat, like she might puke it up, and she instinctively coils her arms around Léon's neck, it's so dark, there's always a newer darkness to fall into—

He jumps.

Chapter 6

Her entire body hurts when they land, a jolt raking through her body, and Millie feels the blood dripping from the shallow scratches on her upper arm, her coat sleeve ruined.

But despite the jolt, she doesn't slam into the bottom of the mine. Léon still has her. When she works to breathe in the darkness, she inhales cold, stagnant air. Léon smells of vanilla and roses, and the gaunt reeked of dried blood. Death. Without any light, that and his arms around her are the most prominent sensations.

That, and a damp odor alongside a distant drip, drip, drip.

Léon helps her stand, which is harder than she anticipated. A wobble of vertigo washes over her brain.

"I can still hear it." His voice is a little strained, perhaps an effect of whatever silver is left in the mine. "When sunrise comes, it'll likely wait for us in the dark little cove, but it can't enter. It's trapped like us."

Millie says, "So both us and it, them, are stuck here for the entire night and day. Great."

Despite the darkness, Léon's eyes are like a cat's, and she faintly makes out him raising a finger. Or a hand. Something. "*At least* an entire day."

"Right. My bad."

Her witch soul whispers, *You know, sarcasm often stems from a fear of authenticity. It's a deflection.*

"It's better than being eaten. Unless you're into that—which, no judgment, of course."

"Of course." Oh, good. At least she won't be kinkshamed down here. "But I'm happy for some company."

Millie can't see much of his expression in the dark, but she thinks it's softened. "As am I."

Standing there without even a shaft of moonlight, she just wants to sleep, but she only has herself to blame for being stuck in a silver mine with a sexy vampire. Putting it like that, it could be a lot worse, but she's still concerned, first and foremost, with how long she can last on a few granola bars. At least she did have that meal.

Léon asks her, "Do you have the ability to produce a fire?"

She stares into the faintly glowing blue eyes. "Can't you see in the dark?"

"Yes, indeed. I was more concerned about your sight."

She sucks in a deep breath. That piece, that shard, stirs. Like an ant on her leg, or the tickle of moth wings. "Hold on. I'm fixing to try something."

"Fixing? What are you fixing?"

Flatly, Millie replies, "Funny. Unless you're not being a smartass, and then it's hilarious."

Even in the darkness, she can tell he's feigning looking abashed. "When have I ever given the impression that I'm anything but utterly serious?"

I've only done this a few times, and it's never big enough to do much. But that shock that came out of me when I faced the gaunt in the tavern...

Again, that stirring. A hand, or some kind of appendage, reaching out, but she's unsure how to clasp it. Maybe she's overthinking it. Maybe she always has. Or maybe her shame has overtaken her; she seems to remember being more attuned to the wings inside her that she sees in the corner of her eyes during fragmented dreams, as fragmented as the entity in her.

Millie shuts her eyes, and somehow, the inside of her lids isn't as dark as her surroundings. Her heart thuds in her ears, loudest in her right. Spots of red, blue, and purple dance in the darkness.

She feels her breaths, that tug in her. At times, she was so desperate to feel it, and other times, she hid it away. She wanted to be a real witch, but she wasn't sure what she'd become once it was all said and done.

Millie stretches her palm out before her, between them, tracing the heat from her chest to her right arm. She sees a fire in her heart, a building tension in her muscles.

The burning scent of smoke, the crackle and pop of a tapering flame, like when she lights a fireplace.

When her eyes snap open, that energy inside her also snaps to life, and a small fire springs up like an opening flower in the center of her palm. She can't help but stare at it in awe that feels a little like fear.

It's never been this simple before.

As if reading her mind, but not, Léon tells her kindly, "You make it look easy." His eyeliner is a little smudged now, and regrettably, it only makes him look hotter. She shouldn't have that on her mind.

I probably shouldn't *have sex with him, but I also probably will.*

Millie eyes him warily. "Is that sarcasm?"

"No."

"Sorry. I know it's not the biggest flame."

A quirk of his mouth. "I suppose there can only be room for one big flame in these mines."

Millie thinks back to what that one guy said at the tavern, what he called Léon. "I mean...I wouldn't call you..."

"I have no shame in it, not anymore." Léon dusts off his dirtied coat. "And about the size of the fire—that's quite all right, Millie." He looks around. She can barely see much in front of her, but as her vision adjusts, she sees faint outlines. As if the witch soul in her is beginning to pour outward. She can feel a yank at her heart, the feeling of life—flora, fungus, something—deeper in the mines. "So long as it helps you. I suppose we might as well make ourselves comfortable."

Comfortable. Château Forgotten Hill Silver Mine, right this way.

Millie tells him, "You know, I forgot to mention this, but nice nails."

"Thank you. I broke one. I tend to prefer the opal and gold colors, but Claire picked this one out. She loves this color. Purples and reds. It's lovely..." He stops, as if remembering to be self-conscious. He looks at her skeptically, as if waiting for her to say more. Something judgmental, maybe, like, *Wait, you're a guy. Why would a guy have nail polish?*

Some part of him expects a demand for an explanation.

Millie shrugs. She hasn't done her nails in a while, of course; even outside of prison, she only painted hers black when she was trying to dissuade herself from chewing on them.

Her aunts would always get her makeup and nail polish for Christmas, and it wasn't that Millie had anything against makeup, but her aunts and mom would chide her for her black, violet, and crimson lipsticks and would exclusively gift her neutral shades to make her look more "classy." It's not that Millie thought there was anything wrong with wearing that sort of makeup, but she always got the sense that her family didn't know her outside of "daughter" and "niece." Except maybe Grandpa, who died too soon, too abruptly in off-white and teal-green hospital rooms.

With little recourse, they explore. She keeps close to Léon, since he can see more of where he's going. They find, where they first landed, a broken elevator shaft.

Millie's throat convulses. The busted elevator is huge, but the way it looks reminds her of the dummy cage she'd get put in for being too stubborn and snapping at the guards because she was tired and throwing up and no, she didn't want to mop the fucking floors tonight; she felt like she was stuck in a cramped, metal coffin.

Or there was that one time, despite how internal and survival-focused she became, Millie showed solidarity for once when a guard had harassed an elderly inmate, and Millie pissed herself, so she'd be reprimanded and punished instead. Non-compliant, useless, disgusting.

They come across a winding metal track with carts, most empty of all but a shiny residue. Millie then inspects another structure on the track, a rectangular wooden structure.

She points at it. "Whoa, is this an outhouse mounted to the track?"

Léon appraises it and nods. "A traveling outhouse. Quite convenient."

They likely would pick it up off the tracks and move it to cover one of the pits they dug throughout the mines. her cheeks flame at the thought of asking Léon to move it for her in one of the excrement pits. She only smells a faint earthy odor nearby.

Millie says, "I guess it's better than nothing, but it looks like the toilet paper has disintegrated." The damp pulp clings to her fingers, the texture sending a shudder through her as she shakes it off. "Well, huh, maybe some of it is salvageable. If I'm desperate enough."

Léon steps over the metal tracks. "Come, I think I hear something that might alleviate any concerns about hygiene." He continues, as she follows, "Sometimes, not every part of the mine was used, especially when it seems that, here, they didn't especially go very far into the process before moving on. And Forgotten Hill, for one reason or another, has a habit of being, hm, being..."

"Forgotten?"

Léon cradles his cheek against a furled hand. "Hence the name, I suppose? Almost like a spell. As if an entire place can have a glamor, except to those drawn to it."

The rocky ground declines under them, the mine feeling more like a labyrinth. She's afraid she won't see a chasm, and she'll plummet.

Eventually, they come across a high cavern of stalactites, with a small opening at the top where moonlight streams down into an amazonite-green, steaming bed of water.

Hot springs.

Huh.

She almost can't believe it.

Millie says, as Léon inspects the pool of water longingly. "Whoa. Nice. Hot springs in the mines?" It feels too good to be true, a feeling she has way too often. She looks around the cavern, able to see better with the moon. The stones are blanketed with a shimmering green moss with blue mushroom sprouts.

Léon says, "It certainly makes for a good natural break room, doesn't it? Though I imagine the conditions were far from luxurious."

"This is pretty ideal, except when I run out of granola bars and starve to death." She's glad Léon bought her that meal.

His expression softens. "You won't starve. We'll figure something out by then. You started this little flame. Have you ever done it before?"

"Not a lot, and I've never had it stay this long."

"Good."

She aches and thinks that it might be nice to shed all her clothes and get into the warm water. She inspects Léon, who's masking his pain well. The back of his coat and tunic are shredded, with blood dripping between his shoulder blades.

Millie winces, her own wounds aching more as she stares at his..

I need to get this all fixed somehow.

"I thought vampires healed almost automatically."

He offers a thin smile. Still so breezily casual even after a near-death experience. It makes her feel as if she knows him; that one aspect reminds her faintly of Fel with her easy lupine grins. "Usually, yes. Gaunts are a little different."

Millie goes over to some of the moss and squints. Extinguishing the fire in her palm, but still feeling a tingle in her hand, she grabs a clump and feels part of her, and the moonlight, and another secret component, seep into it. When she fully stands and looks behind her, Léon is perched on the stones that ring the pool of green water. She approaches him, and as she does, the moss becomes more pliant in her hands.

At his inquiring look, Millie explains to Léon, "This is moon moss. It helps with pain."

"I've never heard of it."

Millie cracks a weak smile. Her head is a bowl of fog. "That's because I made it up."

"Ah. I've heard of witches being able to change ingredients and such with their hands."

"Yeah, that's about all I can do. The magic in me amplifies what healing properties are already there."

"It's a useful skill," Léon says. He's so...agreeable. If only she could shake her damned constant guardedness.

"Now..." She motions for him to show his back to her. "You might want to take off your coat."

Léon offers a sad sigh as he does, folding it beside him. "Matthias gave this to me."

She applies the moss, now more of an uncture, to the scratches on his skin. Despite the hot springs beside her, she shivers. Surely, Léon must notice her hands trembling against him.

"Sorry," she tells him.

"No, you're doing me a favor. Do you need help?" Léon asks. The obvious answer is hell yes, she needs a ton of help. A way out of this mine. A way to clear her name. A way to go to a good therapist and vent for hours. Maybe, then, her hands will stop trembling in that way school bullies would make fun of, that way that made that one teacher go, *Stop shaking your hands. It makes me angry.*

Maybe. Or maybe not.

Léon: "Here, if you make some more, I'll help you with yours."

Millie grunts. "That's okay. I can do it myself."

She has nothing against vampires, really, but she's not sure how safe she is bleeding near him, and she's not sure if he can handle being around a fresh injury.

That said, Léon seems to be managing pretty well, all things considered.

He hangs back until she nods. "I mean, if you really want to."

"If *you* want me to."

"Okay."

We're stuck in this together. Me not trusting him might make our time here longer.

When she gives him more, he applies it gently to her arm. The stinging worsens with contact, and she sucks in a breath

"So, you escaped from prison. That's rather impressive. Good work."

"Thanks. I'll have to put it on my résumé. Cooperative with teamwork. Creative." Well, not that creative. Fel and Simon did most of the work. "Patient."

"I've never been to prison. I would say that I can imagine, but I can't, not entirely."

"I don't know. It was both worse and better than I thought it'd be. We weren't tortured or anything."

"I'd say that's a low bar."

"I guess." Millie heaves a sigh. "I'm not as powerful as I want to be."

"Look at your wound." She does. It's now a faded set of pink lines. Scars. "I'd say you're quite powerful. Give yourself some credit."

"I'm not sure I know how."

"Then, for the time being, I will. You used that rare alchemical component, didn't you?"

"Azoth, yeah. But it's not rare. It's a residue of life."

He gives a wry smile. "I wish I knew what that meant." There's a flicker of recognition, as if he's used to someone explaining things he doesn't entirely understand, but he listens anyway.

"Whenever a butterfly beats its wings or a lizard skitters on a rock, they leave the energy of life—like how we shed cells, which die and regrow. It's everywhere, if you know how to correct it."

"Matthias has used similar metaphors in his research."

Millie looks around. Above, she sees a vein of silver, which Léon keeps his distance from. "How the hell is there a mine that hasn't been stripped of everything it has?"

"Mining wasn't especially prosperous here. Especially in this part of the woods, no one wanted to venture too far. Ventures would start and get abandoned."

"You said that Matthias is powerful. Does that mean he'll find us? I've heard some vampires have psychic bonds to those they love. Can you tell him we need help?"

"I'm trying, but the silver is affecting me. It doesn't hurt unless I touch it, but it's like I'm between a vise." Léon repeats, as if to reassure her, "I'm trying." A distressed crease forms in his brow.

She holds out a hand. "That's okay. Sometimes, it's all you can do."

"Thank you for bearing with me. I wish I were stronger."

"I wish I were, too." She's already said as much, after all. It's not something she'd admit to just anyone. She considers what she's able to do to be a strength in its own right, but she's never felt like she's fully herself. As if there's a locked room inside her, and if she keeps trying, she'll find the key. "You know, you might not be the strongest vampire out there, but you do what you can to protect people. That counts for something."

A few things hold her back from saying more: general anxiety over almost dying; her uncertainty over whether he's into her at all; his two partners; a desire to figure this situation the hell out, even if they're technically safe for now.

Eventually, they settle on a bed of moss by the hot springs. Léon is still sitting as she lies down, her back to him, her head on her rumpled bag.

Her scarred arm nevertheless throbs.

Despite being in a mine trapped by a gaunt and alone with a vampire she barely knows, exhaustion tugs at her eyelids. Momentarily, Millie closes them and releases a small shiver, still cold despite the nearby warmth.

She's always trended toward being cold, and when she sleeps, she falls into a nightmare. And in it, she tumbles down a small, dark tunnel, and there are a hundred eyes.

Chapter 7

When Millie wakes up, she blinks groggily, her eyes aching and dry as she rubs off the gritty crust around them. A weight like a thin blanket is over her. She looks up and sees, no, it's a stark blue. Like Léon's eyes that shine like cobalt headlights in the dark.

His fancy, gold-trimmed coat. Ruined and bloodstained, but still warm. Warmer.

Sometime in the night, Léon must've draped his coat over her. She looks up at the opening. It's day.

She swallows thickly, the moss tickling her hands as she painfully gets to her feet, leaning on a nearby stone for help.

She doesn't have to go far to find Léon on the other side of the cave...counting mushrooms?

"Forgive me," he says, cross-legged near a ring of them. "No cricut. No TV. I was bored."

A vampire in a gold-trimmed Victorian jacket watching TV. It's a funny image.

"Hey, thanks, but if you need your coat back..." Millie resists shaking her head. Of course he needs it back. Even if he's not cold, it's his. She reaches to tug at the collar.

Léon regards her with an emotion she can't quite place. Like pity, but less annoying. "If you need it, you can have it."

"For now, or for good?" She was about to make a joke about keeping it until they both got eaten by gaunts, but she didn't find much humor in her darker thoughts at the moment.

He shrugs and stands. "Either. Perhaps when we get out of here, if I can't mend it—which, admittedly, it looks rather dire in the back—I can give you a replacement."

"One of the coats Matthias has given you?"

"That, or we could have a little shopping trip."

When he, again, sets himself on the edge of the raised pool, Millie decides she has nothing better to do than to press him. "How much do you know about my case? I know it was all the rage for two weeks." The prison should realize she's missing about now. Millie wonders if they actually do release dogs like in movies. Or maybe that's just for murderers. She hopes. She hates the idea of feeling more like a rabbit, meat caught in jaws, than a person.

"I only know that the three of us found it to be very unfair. I was sure that if you hadn't found your way out, Matthias was going to turn into a bat and find a way for you. And Claire was incensed."

"She was mad for a stranger," Millie replies, heart stirring oddly.

"Claire isn't fond of injustice. Whether it's through violence, or neglect."

I didn't find my way out. That was Fel and Simon, and I just left without an explanation of where I was going. Shame bites into her.

Léon explains, "Matthias has been trying to find a cure for the gaunts, and he's been extracting it from different sources of nature. One of the elements he's tried is Azoth, like you have. It's incredibly volatile. I don't understand any of it myself, but from what it sounded like, you'd been making great progress, the closest to finding a solution."

"Closest," Millie points out. "Still failed." A big hurdle was that she didn't necessarily have the means to safely waltz up to a gaunt and say, hey buddy, please don't eat me. Please try this, and we'll hope it cures you instead of making you explode. Thanks!

And eventually, it ended badly, with the police finding her, the sides of her face shredded, blood temporarily blinding her when her head was left hanging in such a way off the side of a set of stairs that it dripped into her eyes.

"Didn't one of the vampires you gave it to improve for a time?"

"Only for 'a time.'"

"That's impressive, nevertheless."

"Close only works in horseshoes and hand grenades." *Shit, I sound like Mom.* If there was a witch who knew more about the properties of Azoth, maybe there'd be more progress. "I'm not a genius. I just have good intuition. And other things."

"What other things? I'm afraid I'm not an expert of magic. If it were me, I'd likely accidentally burn down a good number of buildings if I were a witch. But your magic seems more..."

"Weak?"

"No. It isn't easy, I take it, to manage volatile alchemical elements. Matthias has struggled with it for years. Anything outside of, well, normal chemicals. You aren't weak, but it seems as if a part of you is locked away. Or perhaps that's mere projection."

"I'm not sure if I've locked them away, or if they've locked themselves away. Maybe both."

"'Them'?"

Sitting by Léon near the pool, Millie wraps her arms over herself. "I have a monster in me."

Chapter 8

Léon stares. "What do you mean? Is that figurative?"

"No. You know how a lot of people become witches, don't you?"

"I was under the impression that there were multiple ways. Some through inheritance, others through practicing rites they find in esoteric texts in places like Scholomance and Miskatonic. I must admit, I've spent most of these decades having fun. I don't know as much as I should."

That's fair. What's the point of living forever if you don't you're dour all the time? Millie nods. "Yeah. I guess for me, it's a mix of those. You know what a witch soul is, don't you?"

"Yes, I've heard that witches that have those are especially potent because they have an entity from beyond fueling their power. But it's rare." Léon stares. "You have a piece of one of them in you?"

"I know it's not obvious."

"That could explain why you can handle such volatile matter."

"Yeah. My ancestor fell in love with a demon. Well, she summoned and seduced them, this demon, this fallen angel, so she could have power. And then, they fell in love, so the demon bound themselves to her soul at her request. I think. That's what I was told. Then, fragments of the soul kept getting passed down through her line. Three kids would get three pieces—I don't know how big because they aren't physical. You can't see them."

"How do you know that this entity is a demon?"

"Léon, are you..."

"Dense? That accusation has been levied before."

"Joking. The demon's inside me. That's how I know. I feel them. I know them. Mostly."

Does she?

"Interesting. I must admit that I don't know much about demons. Outside of my early upbringing, of course." Léon palms at the empty space at the hollow of his throat. "If you had a chance, would you rid yourself of the demon?"

Millie frowns, her answer automatic. "No."

"Why not?"

"The good I could do outweighs the bad. And..."

It feels good. Altruism is nice and dandy, but it feels good to have someone there, someone who makes you stronger, even if she hasn't reached her full potential. And it feels wrong to cast the witch soul aside unless they ask her to do so, and then, she would.

Millie says softly, "If only we could connect and become stronger, but I don't know if this shard of them is just so weak after all these years, or if a part of me is holding back." Afraid of what she'd do. What she'd become if she indulged too much in power.

Millie hasn't even asked the witch soul to unlock more of themselves, if they could, though the urge struck her in prison before she grew more resigned.

"Do you love them?" Léon asks, and the question strikes her as odd. Maybe he's thinking of her ancestor, or he thinks some of her reluctance comes from affection.

"No, and they don't love me. They're a part of me, but they feel like a stranger." It's not much different than what she thinks about herself. "They don't—they don't speak to me as often as they did my mom or my granny or anyone before me."

That wasn't the first way she failed in a way that made her mom strangely pleased, but even Mom had admitted that her witch soul was quieter than her own mother's, and Granny certainly never let her forget it, even when she masked the criticism with a pitying smile. Back then, Millie supposed that even immortal beings get tired and depressed. It makes sense. If you're alive for thousands of years, ennui must set in.

"Why is that?" Léon inquires.

"Because we die, and the demon is stuck with the next daughter. They can only leave if there's no one left to inherit, but it's like fate now. I guess it's easier to close everyone out."

Léon rubs under his chin. "You must feel their emotions very deeply."

"I guess I do. I don't even really realize it. Because they don't really feel like a separate part of me anymore. They're just another part of my heart, and it all beats the same."

Contemplatively, Léon replies, "I see. That's a good way of putting it. Poetic. Does this demon have a name?"

Demon.

Ghost. Or haint, as Granny would say.

Witch soul.

Fallen angel.

A fragment of a creature, broken from their fall. Most of the entities that witches bond with are just shards of deadlier creatures. Diminished by pride and punishment, by sullenness, by grief, locked in grief, and then passed along.

And they chose to stay with the one person who wouldn't abandon them, Millie thinks. *Who promised them eternal company, if not with her, then with hundreds more people, until they're so ground down that it's close to oblivion. And how can they not miss her, grieve her?*

"Ezren." Millie doesn't realize she's said it until a shiver rolls down her spine.

They'd been with her since birth, but it was only when she was eighteen and in college and dealing with more than one demon that they sparked. Manifested as another piece of her. Great, another demon to deal with, just as she'd stopped shaving her legs and threw out all her razors to resist the urge to press them to his skin until she formed a shallow pink cut, more of an abrasion.

Léon hums. "There are worse things, I hope Ezren knows, than being bonded with a witch, especially a witty one. At least they know that they'll never be alone."

Part of her thinks that maybe Ezren needs love and understanding, too, and another has mercenary thoughts on what would "unlock" the witch soul/demon/fallen angel to maximize her power.

But she knows, far from being insensitive to Ezren's needs, they want her to use them. To bring them from the morass of her mind into near-life, as broken as they are from being torn asunder by their brethren.

Léon says, "I have a monster in me, too. If I don't restrain myself, I could become like the gaunts. I'm not sure what is worse, thinking about losing myself, thinking of what I could do to those I love, or thinking what would happen if they turned, and I was tasked with killing them out of mercy for themselves and the world."

She frowns. "It's not their fault. The gaunts. Their condition was aggravated by something, something out of their control. I don't know what."

"I don't know either. I worry, though, and I'm perhaps less at risk than the others."

"Claire and Matthias?"

"Yes. They've killed more than me. With Claire, it was always for a reason. With Matthias, I think there was once a point when he lost himself. Loneliness and grief. I think he's relieved to have others around."

"How many people have you killed?"

"Do you mean in the wars I fought, or as a vampire?"

"You..."

"I what?"

"You fought in a war?"

"Two, actually."

Millie stares. "Really?"

"Yes, even someone with my delicate disposition can carry a gun and even, sometimes, shoot it. And sometimes, it even hits its target."

"Okay. Wow. As a vampire, then," Millie clarifies. "You can tell me your war stories later, if it's too much."

"It's not..." Léon goes quiet, and Millie doesn't push him to keep speaking. She can't even fathom what he went through. Eventually, he says, "Technically, two and a half."

"What do you mean?"

"Besides war, I've killed two and a half people."

Millie stares, and she asks warily, "And a half?"

"Well, I bit deeply in the man's throat, but it was my wife who ripped out his jugular. Technicalities."

Though she doesn't know what Claire looks like, the image is visceral. Millie wonders what sort of person rips out someone's jugular and goes on living, having done that. Her throat swells. *Could I do that?* "Christ."

"No. Not really." A little forlorn. Léon sets a hand on his collarbone.

Millie asks, "Why did you two do that?"

His jaw tenses, but his voice is soft. Genuine. "They hurt my wife. That's all I can say. She wanted them dead, and I wanted to be there for her. For bloodlust, but also for support when all was said and done."

"Supportive bloodlust," Millie says dryly, rubbing her aching chest, which has suddenly gotten uncomfortably hot, like she has a fever.

Despite the heat, chills unfurl down her arms.

"Exactly. That was the only time I've killed, almost a hundred years ago. If we hadn't killed them, we would've been slain, and perhaps worse, before they decided to put us out of our collective misery. When I saw Claire rip out a man's jugular, all I could think was, by God, I love her. I love her. I love her. I love her."

Normally, Millie would hear a man say he loved his wife when he watched her murder someone, and she'd think, *What the fuck?*

But she also knows that sometimes you have to protect yourself when everyone else—law enforcement, a culture that blames you for your abuse—has failed. You have to kill.

Besides, if she had a wife who ripped out an evil person's throat, she'd probably fall in love again, too.

It's not pretty; Léon isn't devilishly smirking. He looks off plaintively, eyes half-lidded.

And Claire—Millie can only hope she found a little peace back then knowing the men who hurt her were dead.

Léon asks her, "Do they, this entity, ever take you over, so you can't control yourself?"

Millie can't help how her eyes widen in horror. "No."

He shakes his head. "I don't mean to frighten you, or insult you."

"You haven't. I just...if I ever spoke fully with Ezren, I'd want us to be partners, not one dominating the other." She looks at Léon, the bluish shadows forming under his eyes. "You must be really hungry. or thirsty. however it works."

Léon offers a reassuring smile that makes her heart flutter. If he's bothered by the change of subject, he doesn't show it. "I'll live. I've already died, after all."

"I'm not entirely sure how that works. Can you ever starve?"

"Enough to make me miserable. Not enough to kill me. That is much harder, though I suppose, not too terribly hard if anyone finally resisted my charms and had the urge."

"And your death in your first life...Matthias, he had to kill you both, didn't he?"

"He didn't have to. Perhaps we might've killed each other, but I couldn't do it. Or perhaps we might've taken our own lives. But he did. He could've let us remain mortal, but he did what we wanted. What we asked."

Millie's frown deepens. "I just...I just can't understand being with someone who did that to you. Who has that capacity to do that to you. He still had to do that, and then watch you die, not knowing if it'd work."

Léon regards her grimly. "Yes. But we went to him demanding for it to be done. It's not often that one in this world gets to choose who kills them. Better there than in the gutter. it wasn't murder; it was release. Freedom. We wanted a new start."

"Yeah, I think I get it," Millie says, mostly to be agreeable. She can't quite wrap her head around killing someone she cares about.

"I traded all my shame for this." No shame. Millie struggles to imagine that.

"And do you ever regret it? Do you ever feel like it'd be better to be human?"

"No. never. It's a cliche, I know, to realize that it's better to die, but the world always wanted me dead, and I'll be damned if I ever give it that satisfaction. I died, so I could live. When I was human, I was angry all the time, though the opium dulled it. made me in denial. Opium and sex. In truth, I wanted to eat the world for what it did to me."

"What stopped you, or Claire?" Millie is skeptical, given what Léon has already admitted.

"The two of us would've done well devouring the world. That's what two flames together do: They burn brighter and consume. Matthias, though, he was tired. We wanted new lives, but he wanted one, too. a quiet one. I'm not entirely certain he got what he ordered."

"I mean, it's nice, having someone around to talk to. or listening, even when you have nothing to say."

"Yes. Perhaps you could reach out to Ezren, and he can help you."

"Help us."

"I don't only mean our current predicament, but yes."

She hates the idea of, as Léon said it casually enough, using Ezren as "fuel." Fueling her power.

Do I hate it? Mom hated it. Spoke of the monster inside her that should've been exorcized.

Léon tells her with earnest humor, "I like when everyone else around me is stronger than me. When they aren't, it means I must do more, and well, I prefer leaving *solving* problems to others. Now, causing problems, we can talk about that. That is to say, if you find a way to unleash your power, I completely support it."

Millie arches a brow. "You want me to act more like a demon?"

"Do *you* want to act more like a demon?"

"I want it. I just, sorry, I need a moment."

Scared at what she'll unleash. What she'll become.

Ezren has gotten too quiet, quieter than usual, quieter than her heartbeat. She needs to check on them.

Is that really why you care? Your ancestors were worthy. Are you?

I don't want this for them. I want it for me.

But wanting something for herself feels even more dangerous than what landed her in a cell.

"Is there anything I can do?" Léon asks her.

Millie reaches out, and he grasps her hands, rubbing a thumb over her knuckle.

"Of course, my witch."

"Funny. When you say it, it doesn't sound like a replacement for a meaner word."

Chapter 9

Night comes, another day passes. Léon, as her only company, keeps her from losing herself when she swears she hears claws and skittering above them, and her throat tightens and her hands shake. Her back is on fire.

They must get out of here soon.

And then night arrives again, and as Léon's gently pacing footfalls and the water soothe patterns into her head, Millie dreams.

She's on the first floor of her university library, right outside of the rare books room, where she once found a nineteenth century copy of John Keats' poems and couldn't stop from hopping in place. But when she enters, it isn't the same room; nevertheless, it's an old library or study of some sort where she can barely see the damasque wallpaper for the dark, ceiling-high shelves of books lining most of the room. There are oil paintings everywhere, one of a lighthouse in a storm. Cobwebs hang from the ceiling. A hearth blazes, and above it, a dead-eyed elk head glowers down at her.

A plush armchair sits with its high back to her.

In this dream-realm, she's wearing a long, deep blue overcoat over a long black dress. She tugs her coat over herself and takes a deep breath.

The air hums like a spell, or a prayer.

From the armchair stems long, slithering tendrils of glittering magic, which curl over the red carpet and around her feet like starry blades of grass. She sees wings with hundreds of feathers that look more like prismatic slicks of oil. But they are not high and proud; they droop on the armrests, broken and limp, and the air smells of smoke. Not the woodsmoke of the fireplace; brimstone.

Millie approaches and comes to the side of the chair.

Ezren. Their face is hard to describe. Faces, rather, the most prominent one shaped vaguely like a lion's snout and mane, with floating hairs of a color she can't describe, like a rose-gold-lilac.

They have eyes and mouths that shift like rain on a window pane. Their skin is translucent and seems to swallow part of the fire, which swirls in their face and wings. Little universes.

Millie's not afraid of them. On the contrary. She feels mournful. She regrets this situation, though she had no say in it. Neither of them have control of their bodies. How much of Ezren is left since whatever damned them for good?

There's a difference between a promise when it's made and years upon years from then.

Ezren didn't love *her*. Whatever love means to them. They were here to fulfill an old promise, a promise so powerful it transcends centuries. Does time mean anything to a corrupted angel?

Now, they're withdrawn, sullen, and Millie understands. She might want the power of a witch, yes, but she doesn't know how to access it, and she doesn't want to do it in any way that might hurt or control this resident in her.

And then, if she were to hurt anyone else...

With every descendent, a piece of the witch-entity dies. She wonders if she were to try to hold Ezren if they would crumble to ashes in her hands.

They are a part of me, and I'm a part of them. If I destroy them, I destroy myself.

"Is this what you want?" Millie whispers to them. "Just for someone to see you?"

A rasp, like sea salt over stones. "I've always been here for you to see." A gray eye floats to the surface of Ezren's cheek to stare at her.

"But I've never really looked." Because of fear. Because of shame. "I don't know. I guess I just really wanted to respect your privacy."

Ezren releases a noise between a scoff and a laugh. She can't tell which mouth it comes out of. "I can't tell if you're joking."

"I'm sorry you've been lonely and stuck for so long. I think I feel that way, even when someone's around. No matter how many times I'm told that I'm not alone."

"Could you leave if you wanted?" Millie asks.

"I've left those in your family that didn't want me around, yes, even at the cost to myself. Hidden, waiting for the spell, the promise to take hold again."

Millie takes in their words. "I see."

Ezren asks her, "*Do* you want me to leave?"

"No. Stay. I want to hear you out. There's so much I know, and so much I don't."

Ezren isn't a monster, and if they are, so is she, and that's okay. Often, people are monsters, and so, monsters are people. monsters can fight. monsters can protect. monsters can love. she—she and Ezren, she and Léon, and maybe even his companions—she belongs with them, and they with her. How didn't she see it before?

In this hazy and liminal world, that means more than her fear.

Still, it was always easier, and harder, to be alone.

Millie continues to stand there, not sure what to do or say. "What happened? Who was...no one's even told me her name. Who was she?"

"Her name was Mercy. Mercy O'Brien, from Derry. A sad widow with eyes just like yours. Alone, I wept and wiped away tears and blood from angel-flesh in a fae-wood. I mourned the loss of my brethren; when I lived in heaven, I spent so many lazy hours warm and content nestled with thousands of my family. Being held, and being enough."

A long pause. The fire in the hearth pops and hisses.

"And then, I had no one, a mocking emptiness where God once was, a silenced scream, And she answered. She found me, and she gave me a home, tended to my burning wounds with crushed petals of pot marigold. When English soldiers tried to intimidate her, she needed help. She needed company. So, I gave her power and lived with her for seven decades."

"What happened to the soldiers?"

That one eye sinks back into the abyss of their not-flesh. "We slew them in secret with nightmares and fever-curses, and after she made love to me with every inch of us slathered in blood and organs, we lived in peace. We were grieving and hateful creatures, cynical to love, but she was my home, and I hers. She would sing and thread bog rosemaries and clovers into my hair. Then, at age one-hundred and six, she grew very ill. Her hair thinned; she had trouble breathing. She coughed blood and became nothing but bone. I would feed her corned beef and lentil soup, until she could no longer eat. I would wipe away her sick and press a warm cloth to her brow. I wrapped her in her favorite quilt and rested her chin on my shoulder as we sat on her favorite green hill, amid wild strawberries and dandelions.

"Her ribs cut into me. She shivered, and sobbed, and died, but before she died, and I buried her under a hazel tree, she promised that I would never be alone. So, I was passed down along your bloodline. Some ignored me, except for my power. Others ignored me completely, so I turned away to think, and sit, and dream. Unknown to every living thing, except the one who cared, so long ago."

When Millie tries to reply, she chokes, the pain of unshed tears pounding in her head. She has the feeling that they're keeping from crying, too.

Once she speaks, she croaks out, "I'm sorry. I've been wanting to see you. To know you, but I just..."

"Have you? I think you are afraid of me. Of what I might make you."

They're right. Or they were. For so long, she's been driven by that pinch in her stomach, that tightness in her chest and throat. And when she wasn't, when she was bold, she was punished for it. Proven right, or wrong, she's not really sure.

Millie is tired of all that.

"Ezren. Look at me." She reaches out, moving in front of them, where she cannot quite tell how many limbs they have, or where they end.

They shift their face.

More eyes stare at her, and they are stranger and more beautiful and somehow recognizable.

Their face is now a series of blue-ish whorls that rise to meet her offered hands, with the twin suggestion of golden cat-eyes and an ever-spiraling stream of gold and silver hair. A mane, the hint of a lion's snout, but a body in a vague humanoid form with tapering arms.

She's not entirely sure if she truly can touch them, or if they will flow out of her fingers like vapor.

But when her fingers settle, it's like touching warm water. Like the start of a good, long bath. Or how the hot springs must feel like.

Millie murmurs, "I—I'm sorry. I know you loved her, and I'm sorry she's gone." She wonders if anyone has told them that over the hundreds of years. An acknowledgment. Did anyone give Ezren an apology for however they fell, whether they cavorted with flaxen-haired Lucifer in a meadow or some other cosmic happenstance Millie can't even grasp?

Ezren leans close, and so does she.

Millie aches to be touched. She remembers the haze of desire. There was that time before she moved to college, in her childhood home that smelled like a rosy convent, when she masturbated while listening to *The Fame Monster*. There was the time when she broke up with Simon, and she kissed another man at a bar, and she took him to her new, small apartment and let him fuck her. And despite saying she wasn't religious anymore, she was filled with guilt after, like she'd betrayed someone.

And then, in the long, insomniac nights in prison, she'd touch herself as covertly as possible and imagine her witch soul reaching out.

But it felt wrong, and she stopped. If Ezren didn't want to speak to her, to touch her, even her fantasies felt cruel.

Now, she feels one of their appendages gliding over her side and behind her back, in a sort of embrace.

When they kiss, the sky and clouds and sea all melt against her lips, salt and ozone and Godflowers. Wild strawberries and a hot fudge sundae after a long day. She wants them around her like a blanket.

Soon, she gets her wish as they rise, and so does she, her feet lifting off the carpet. She's suspended there while their cupped wings and tendrils form a warm cradle for her body. She spreads her legs and realizes that she's naked, and they're naked, and she wants more. She wants completion in their mingled love and grief. She deepens the kiss as these feathers and tendrils tickle her skin, and one of Ezren's appendages gently trails from her jaw to the column of her throat, as she breaks the kiss to arch back. Ezren wraps her close, and another part slips into her.

More more more.

At once, Ezren teases her clit and pumps into her, and they vibrate while the hum in the air intensifies, and they emit strong, deep purrs that rattle the room. She writhes and grabs, grabs, grabs at angel hair and nebulas.

They swell inside of her, as big as a fist, so she's lost in a haze of pain and pleasure.

We're both bones and stars. They're filling me with stars.

She loses sight of where they end, and she begins.

It doesn't take long for her pleasure to mount, and crest, and she peers into a hundred kaleidoscopic eyes and feels seen.

Fire floods her, fire as hot as magma and cold as frost; she burns with flames and ice, and she's not sure which burns brighter.

Millie wakes up covered in sweat, the space between her thighs damp. She lies there for a good while, taking long, deep breaths. She still tastes smoke, and she swallows and finds comfort in it. She's both tired and rejuvenated with that lazy pleasure she feels when she's resting in bed after sex, that moment when the tension in her stomach unspools.

And the fire in her...

She's no longer cold.

When she rises, it doesn't take long to find her friend-in-forced-proximity. Léon is sitting in the steaming water, still wearing his clothes, his cheek nestled in his palm as he leans an elbow on a stone.

"Nerves," is his explanation. It must be difficult for him to admit that with how easy his demeanor usually is. Though the silver doesn't hurt unless there's direct contact, it's still an inconvenience for him. She wonders if there's a way to help.

Millie nods in understanding and climbs in to sit across from him.

"You don't have to," Léon tells her, too late. "I worry that you'll get cold with your clothes wet."

Not only my clothes, Millie almost says, still wearing his ruined jacket. "It's okay. I don't think I'll feel cold anymore." The fire spreads within her, thrumming in her blood. It comforts her and yet makes her antsy to act. To let it out. All her fingers twinge.

After they bask in companionable silence, Léon straightens, lowering his hand and facing her fully. "Are you all right? You seem to be pondering something."

Faintly, Millie says, "I just had sex with Ezren in my dream."

Léon's reaction has no judgment. There's slight mirth and something else, a hesitation as he processes what she's told him. "I see. And you..."

She trudges over to join him, sitting beside him. Veins of light dance on the stone walls and his face, the silver lines glinting, but not as much as his eyes in the near-dark, which is no longer as hard to see in. "I saw them, and they saw me."

Léon muses. "Well, if we're on the subject, was it good?"

She holds his stare. "Yes. Very. I feel different."

"Are you all right?"

"Yes. How much is it a turnoff that I have a fallen angel inside me?"

"None at all. One of my lovers, after all, was on the precipice of becoming a gaunt once, and he can change into a form close to it."

"Matthias?"

"Yes."

Millie feels bold. After all, he asked about how it was with Ezren. "Has he? For you? Turned into that to be with you?"

"Yes."

"You liked it?"

He laughs. It's a pretty sound, pretty and sweet; she wants to taste his sweetness like honey. "It was different, but yes."

Millie cranes her chin. He's quite a bit taller than her, so even when he sits, there's a difference. She plunges her hand in the water and, in the heat, finds his hand, tentatively curling her fingers around his and anticipating him to retract from the touch.

The air between them is heavy and hot.

Damp, scarred, and disheveled, they surge together. She breaks the handhold to get into his lap, and as he lets her get on top, Léon wraps his arms around her back when their lips meet, feverish and insatiable. She presses and presses, and his fangs nick her bottom lip.

"Je suis désolée," Léon mutters, pulling back.

"It's okay," Millie tells him, kissing him again, and he reciprocates. She tastes her own blood and lets it fall on his tongue. Her hips piston against his.

When the kiss breaks again, Léon looks at her through pretty, half-lidded eyes. "You *are* different."

"Yeah." She had no idea her witch soul—Ezren—could feel so good. So content.

He raises a single finger. "Not that I like to talk—"

"Right, right."

"But I just want to ensure that this is you." Millie understands. For so long, another reason she feared allying with this part she buried in her—while they also buried themselves far away and locked the door—was because she was unsure what darker parts were her or Ezren. It extended to other things, too. She disappointed her mom by being a bisexual "unnatural freak."

Unnatural freak? You passed a demon to me on my eighteenth birthday, and you're worried that I'm gay?

Her mom, who'd also had Ezren locked away in her head, who also was once more open until she became a "true" lady.

And so, when Millie started not relating to some aspects of femininity—the shock and disappointment Mom gave her over the smallest things, like saying her favorite color was now purple, not pink—she wondered what liminal parts of her *were* her. After all, everyone else in town, who went to one of the three Baptist churches on her street, would say she's possessed by a demon.

"Yes, it's me," she tells Léon.

"Millie, I understand, and I hope that I don't sound patronizing, but I'm not sure if either of us is ready for this. Now, don't get me wrong. I quite love having sex, and you are very beautiful, but I think perhaps we should consider this when we both feel safer."

Maybe she might've found it frustrating and patronizing years ago when even the slightest doubt in others about her choices felt like a full-blown criticism. Felt like her mom sneering at her all over again. But she's actually touched that he's taking their situation into account. That if they ever start a relationship, make love, either or both, they should do it in a comfortable environment. She hasn't even processed what happened in her dream, if it was only a dream.

Besides, she can't entirely explain it, but she feels like that time she popped two potent weed gummies into her mouth and, within thirty minutes of watching *The Holy Mountain*, felt like she was rocketing to another solar system. That, but a hundredfold.

"Okay. I hear you. You're right. We don't have to. But maybe you could..."

"What is it?"

"I think you should bite me. I don't know how to explain it, but it's like there's been a dam in me, and it's broken, and if you drink my water, we might be able to find a way out of here. If I can share my power, I don't know what will happen, I'm a little freaked out, but I think that it's worth a shot."

"You might feel disoriented from even minor blood loss. I'm unsure a granola bar is enough to keep you from fainting, if it's too much, and after what you've endured. Especially one so paltry, and with, of all things, raisins."

Millie jokes, "Sorry if my blood is raisin flavored."

"Now, that would be a true cause for apology! Thankfully, food doesn't influence the taste, but I'm not worried about that. I don't want to hurt you."

"I know, but I trust you. they trust you."

With her last words, she's not sure if she means Ezren, or Matthias and Claire, who must surely be waiting to hear from Léon. Who might finally be able to hear from him should he drink from her and gain even a bit of Ezren's power. That's all she can think of to nullify the effects of the surrounding silver.

With lowered eyelids, he presses a soft kiss to her forehead. Still in his lap, she raises her chin to set her temple against his, her companion in this desperate, dark moment. She cannot help but imagine her, him, and Ezren in a frenzy of kaleidoscope-feathers and appendages embracing them as they all kiss. Ezren's mouths and tendrils on and in them both, flowering and making them bloom.

Millie leans back, pushing her thick curls back to expose her throat. Shutting her eyes, she doesn't see Léon open his mouth, but she feels his hair tickle her collarbone, feels his lips latch onto the side of her neck. She becomes aware of her hummingbird pulse, and then a stinging pain.

The prickle, which momentarily makes her tense, gives way to a rush of intense ecstasy, a tingle spreading through her arms, legs, and groin. The flames in her writhe and pool in her throat, surging from her into him, as she, as they pump into and enter Léon. It takes all her strength not to moan as he feeds, until he draws away with a final lick, as if kissing the wound better.

When he's done, a wave of dizziness crashes into her, but then passes. He keeps her upright with both hands above her elbows, his eyes earnest with sympathy. "Will you be okay?"

Millie smiles. "Yeah. That felt better than I thought it would. It felt great. I could get used to it."

Léon shuts his eyes, and the air seethes and hums around them.

Minutes pass, and Millie tries, even with the blood in him, to strengthen his powers through will alone. No, not just will. Ezren is thriving and alive, and they're augmenting her power.

When her companion opens his eyes, he tells her, "I hear them."

"Who? Claire and Matthias?"

"Yes. I told them everything. They're coming, but the gaunt will be waiting for us."

"All right. How soon will your companions be here?"

"Sooner than you might think."

Despite being soaking wet, after Millie retrieves her bag, they rush back to the mine entrance. Or under it, rather, with the broken elevator.

Millie whispers, curling a hand over her heart, "Ezren, I know I'm new at this, but I need you."

A tug on her heart. Her soul. She stands firm. Léon's hand slips into hers, and she squeezes it.

Metallic creaking and scraping as the elevator slowly repairs itself.

It's a pretty big elevator that might've at one time, fit dozens of workers, but still, she flashes back to the sting of pepper spray in her mouth, curling beside a floor grate where it was easier to breathe...

Enough.

Jaw firm, she says to Léon, "Let's go."

They do.

Chapter 10

When they exit the mine in haste, it's the dead of night, and they're surrounded by tall pines, the stars only visible in the small clearing. Millie expects to be immediately accosted by the gaunt, and her heart jolts when a shriek pierces the woods.

The gaunt is there, but it's not alone—there's another, much bigger one that doesn't quite look like the rest—it's less gray and more silver—entirely silver. And though she isn't close, she sees that even its eyes are gray and near-pearlescent with the shuddering light from the full moon.

No, not its. His. Him. Matthias bears down on the smaller gaunt, snapping his dagger-teeth at it. What strikes Millie the most, however, is the woman with dark, curly blonde hair who rides atop Matthias. She's dressed in black leather with chainmail over her chest. A black bag swings from one arm, a sword at her opposite hip. A *sword*.

Oh.

Millie's heart skips a beat, and she stares breathlessly at the woman, and when she looks at Léon, she sees something that echoes her own feelings, albeit with more intensity. Relief. Passion. Adoration.

Seized by an urge that's unsure is entirely her own, Millie runs to where the woman dismounts and, having taken the blade into her hand, swings it down, slicing off a part of the smaller gaunt's ear.

Meanwhile, coming close to where claw marks leave scores in the earth, she extends her hand, and she's pushed back by the plume of fire that spirals out of her palm and hits one of the gaunt's back legs as Matthias bears down, snapping at its throat.

But in the end, it's the woman who—maneuvering under the creature, with too much to focus on between its three assailants—violently shoves the blade forward and drives it directly into the gaunt's heart.

It screams, and shudders, and slumps, as the woman removes the blade, and blood spurts and darkens the grass and silt. The air feels with the stenches of blood and burning flesh.

Millie's throat constricts, as she watches the gaunt die and hears Léon's footfalls, feels that slight tremor that she might not have heard before. A heart draining, and dying.

The woman, lost in the lust of battle, licks her sword and then bends to feed ravenously at the dead beast's wound.

Will killing and feeding on gaunts turn these normal vampires into gaunts, or are these creatures far too gone to be considered a mark on their souls?

Maybe. Maybe not. Nonetheless, vampires are people, and gaunts were once vampires. Léon could turn into one of these monsters one day.

She stares at the dead creature. *This is a person. We're all people. I have to find a solution to all of this. I need to rest, to get better, and fix all this. Will you help me?*

Yes, Ezren says, his voice fanning across her brain.

Lost in the overwhelming moment and the assault on her senses, Millie hears the rustle of bushes, and a silver-haired man in a white tunic and black pants emerges, with the bag over his shoulder. Matthias. In the frenzy, after the gaunt died, she must've missed him transforming back and, nude, going to dress in relative privacy. Approaching the woman and the dead gaunt, he raises a hand, as if to touch the woman's back, but she stiffens and backs away from the growing pool of blood, as if remembering herself, though she's already drenched with blood.

Eyes bright, she turns, her attention falling on Léon. She rushes to swing her arms around his neck and presses her nose against his, smearing his face with blood. He doesn't seem to mind as he hugs her, smiling into their passionate, ruddy kiss.

Until, as if feeling two people watching them, the woman looks at Millie for the first time and offers an apologetic grin. Her voice is light. "I'm sorry. This is terribly rude of me, where are my manners? My name is Claire. You must be Millie." Clotted gore smatters her mouth, chin, and throat, like that time Millie was little and got into the blackberry jam.

Claire.

Is this really Claire? Millie feels both drained of blood in her face and so, so warm. Léon spoke so well about her, and yet, she had no idea that Claire would be *this* lovely, even drenched in blood.

Dizzy at the odor of blood, Millie's too tired yet pumped by her new powers to feel inadequate—she isn't. But she's struck by how different she is from this ethereal trio, undead but passionate and furious and alive.

"Yeah. Um. Hi," Millie manages, and Matthias approaches. He looks over Léon, who stares with half-lidded intensity, and the vampires enter a three-way embrace as Matthias presses one palm into Léon's back and leans to nudge his forehead tenderly, like an affectionate cat, and Claire holds them both.

Millie can only shuffle her feet and wait.

When the moment ends, Matthias steps back and looks Léon up and down. "You're all wet."

Léon gives a mock pout. "Oh, come now. It's not the first time."

Matthias gives a sound like a scoff. "Yes, you're fine." But, moving to inspect, he nevertheless looks with concern at Léon's back, his shredded tunic, and gently touches the skin near one of the new scars.

Léon offers a small smile and flips back his hair, sharing a gaze with both Millie and Claire. "You know I do so *love* to play the damsel in distress every once in a while. It really helps a fellow feel wanted."

All at once, ennui floods Millie. She's too aware of how separate she is from the three of them, even as Claire regards her with an emotion she's too tired to read.

Millie wants a long bath and a hot meal and a warm bed. She wants to leap into Léon's arms and kiss him and comb her fingers through his golden curls.

And then, maybe, she can decide what they are and what she'll do with her life.

More than that, she wants to know why seeing a man who turned into a bat monster and a woman drenched in blood doesn't make her afraid for long, but instead stirs the space below her navel.

Her stomach growls, and she winces. She hopes no one takes notice, but she's with three vampires, so all six eyes fall on her. Millie flashes an awkward smile, too overwhelmed by the bloody scene to feel self-conscious about her coffee-stained teeth.

How must she look, disheveled and wearing Léon's beautiful blue coat?

Matthias regards her seriously. Then again, it seems to be that seriousness is the only way he regards anything, so far. "You're the one who saved him."

"We saved each other, I think." Her cheeks grow warm. If only these two, Matthias and Claire, knew what's happened, what went on inside her dream.

If only she could use her new fire to burn away her shame, that relic of a Catholic upbringing.

Matthias, Count Matthias says, "At home, I'll make something for you, but I fear we don't keep regular food here. It won't take long, however, for me to buy a few meals for now. Tell me what you want." The air he gives off is regal, and even if he doesn't mean to be pushy, his words sound like a command.

Her heart aches. *Home.*

"Soup," Millie tells Matthias.

The silver-haired vampire stares. Not one to be intimidated, Millie nevertheless struggles to read his expression. "What kind of soup?"

"Tomato soup, with a grilled cheese sandwich." It's easy enough, but she's not sure how often a vampire would cook for anyone and know recipes.

He gives her a nod, and then, soaked in differing amounts of water, sweat, and blood, they are on their way. Millie gives one last look at the dead gaunt, as they leave it behind.

One day, I'll find the answer.

Chapter 11

Thankfully, rather than walking the rest of the way or getting into a horse-drawn carriage, Claire offers to drive. On a lonely forest road, rather than finding a hearse, they all get in a four-seat, wine-red Ferrari that, while sleek, looks like a much older model. From the 1970s or 80s, maybe. If Millie cared about cars, which she doesn't.

Already woozy from not having a hearty meal in a while, to keep from feeling sicker, she gets in the passenger seat beside Claire. She wonders what a stranger might think if they could see past the darkened windows, and they witnessed a driver with a bloodstained mouth.

Once they reach their destination, Millie stares at the manor on the hill in awe. It is a pointed mass of dark gray stone with a vermillion roof. A new wave of wakefulness hits her, like when hours of sleeplessness turn into a surreal bout of energy right before the crash.

Predictably, on this hill by the sea, as she faintly hears ocean waves, there's a lot of stairs with a fancy fountain and mournful statues, not all of them human. Going up to the vast entrance, replete with a wolf-head knocker, Millie stumbles.

Claire stops, and she and Léon help steady her. "Oh, are you all right?"

"Yeah," Millie replies, and when they enter the main hall, it's a giant crimson gullet. A gargoyle stares down, and the entire hall of dark floral wallpaper is lined with various oil paintings. Some of beautiful landscapes, others of classical scenes like nymphs in water or a dark-haired woman standing mournfully in a cornfield at dusk, a tear track on one cheek.

Millie thinks of those lines from one poem: *Through the sad heart of Ruth, when, sick for home, / She stood in tears amid the alien corn...*

But in the distance, where the corn parts like golden hair, another woman is there, carrying a basket. Naomi, perhaps.

Where you go, I will go; where you lodge, I will lodge; your people shall be my people, and your God my God. Where you die, I will die—there will I be buried.

Self-consciously, Claire says, eyes on Millie, "We should get washed up."

Millie starts, looking at Matthias, and then at the fearsome gargoyle, "Is it okay if I..."

"Yes, yes," the Count says, looking off to the side with those imperceptible quicksilver eyes, "you're free to use this downstairs washroom and bedroom. We can speak after you eat and you've rested, and we can try to repay you."

She tries to hide her wince as her stomach painfully grumbles again. Presumably, the meal will come after her companions—her *hosts* aren't blood-covered. "Try to repay me? For what?"

And what does he mean "try"? As in, he might attempt it and fail? Or that he might not be able to compensate her enough for what she's done?

"For protecting Léon," he intones.

"I mean, we saved each other. It's nothing."

Matthias stops, and his voice carries a hard edge. "No, it isn't nothing." A pause, and his tone eases somewhat. "We don't have many guests, but I do keep supplies for mortal visitors. I can make you your soup and sandwich soon enough."

He's *making* the tomato soup? She's touched because she just expected it right out of the can. Put it in a pan and heat it up for five minutes.

With that, they leave her, but not before Léon takes her hand again, and she gives him a smile.

As she waits, Millie finds the dining room easily enough, through two arches to the right of the main hall. It's a long, rectangular room. The mahogany table, with its burgundy lace tablecloth, has two chairs at both ends and six on each side.

A cornucopia with fake yellow and orange gourds sits atop an unlit hearth, which boasts a pine garland with clear lights. Festive. She can't remember the last time she really celebrated the holidays.

The entire room smells faintly of tallow, and indeed, there's candelabras—fucking candelabras like out of an old movie!—on the walls. A cobweb sways in one ceiling corner.

She goes to sit at the end nearest to the fireplace, but stops and, curious, walks through another arch to find a surprisingly small kitchen with a stone floor. The counters are slate gray, and when she opens the fridge, there's indeed a few supplies. Vegetables and cheeses.

She wonders if Matthias makes dinners for himself, Claire, and Léon, even though the tastes aren't as robust for immortals. Maybe it's the domestic routine that counts. The freezer section is full of different meats, and the cupboards have different broths. And the stove, well, it looks electric, maybe, but it looks more like a white and black chest of drawers than a modern stove.

At the end of the row of counters is a black chest freezer. When she opens it, it's understandably stuffed full with blood bags.

Her curiosity sated, she returns to the dining room and sits at the head of the table. Though a chill lingers in the air, she doesn't feel cold; she has Ezren, and they have her. She waits about twenty minutes before she hears rustles and clanks in the kitchen.

The bowl Matthias gives her is as big as her head, and he gives her a separate plate with the sandwich. The silverware is, well, definitely not silver. Millie's mouth waters when she smells the butter and sees the cheeses dripping off the slices of toasted bread.

It almost distracts her from noticing the white apron Matthias has wrapped around himself.

"What cheeses are these?" Millie asks, pointing to the grilled cheese.

"Gruyere and cheddar."

Millie hasn't even heard of the first one. "What are these green little spices on top of the bread?"

"Thyme and rosemary," he replies. Uncertainty flashes in his eyes. "I'll leave you—"

"I really appreciate you doing this for me."

He stares, as if unsure. "I'm glad."

"This looks and smells good. Really, really good."

She expects his steely exterior to crack. No such luck. In fact, his reply is almost haughty.

"Of course it is. I wouldn't cook you a terrible meal." His tone is so dry that Millie's not sure if she imagines the humor.

Is Matthias always so curt? Is she imagining that tinge of irritation she's used to from growing up with her mom?

Curt. Rude. Like Millie can talk. She imagines after hundreds of years, you stop dressing up your words, if you ever did in the first place.

No, maybe he's being funny. Maybe she's overanalyzing, as usual. Maybe he, like her, is on the spectrum, and what's rude to a lot of people just feels like blunt truth or common sense or objective truth. He made a meal, and he wouldn't do it badly.

"Thanks," she says to him before he leaves.

His gray eyes remain serious. "Of course."

The tomato soup is buttery on her tongue and bursts with the sweet clove taste of basil and a salty hint of parmesan.

She tears apart the grilled cheese slices to dip them into the soup and is surprised that, amid the creamy swirl of tomatoes and mild cheeses, she tastes yellow onions caramelized in brown sugar, alongside hints of mayonnaise and olive oil. Who puts onions in grilled cheese sandwiches?

Apparently Matthias, and hell, it's good. No, it's exquisite. The sumptuous flavors mingle in her mouth. Oh, she can definitely get used to this. She can't wait to introduce Matthias to Pinterest.

It's only after she's mostly finished that she thinks about the leap of trust it took to let a stranger cook for her, much different than ordering her own food at the tavern with Leon across from her.

Also, this is way better than microwaved mac and cheese or a soggy grocery store salad.

Millie'd been around two-hundred and ten pounds when she went into prison, and she lost nearly forty in six months. While she'd never really been skinny (whatever "real skinniness" is), which her mom mentioned constantly, she felt more hollow in prison, not just existentially, but the way her thighs and stomach felt as they thinned. She thinks that she'll enjoy having a fancy vampire make her meals, and regardless of what she looks like, maybe she'll feel more like herself again.

Good things happen when she just lets people do things for her. When she lets them in.

Speaking of which, Léon comes and sits beside her once she's done.

Millie tells him, "I thought vampires didn't really taste food that's not blood. So, I'm surprised he would cook for me, I guess."

A little self-conscious at how she tore apart and inhaled her meal, she presses the folded crimson cloth napkin to her lips and suppresses a burp.

Léon grins and waves a hand. "Oh, ever since we had a TV installed, he watches all those cooking shows." She guesses a cool thing about being immortal is having time to be good at a lot of things and learn a lot of languages. Imagine being able to know at least ten languages and still have time to learn more, while being able to learn how to paint, write, cook, knit, and so on. "He's hopeless when we try to get him to watch shows, like that one with the dragons that ended horrendously, but he absorbs anything with information on whatever task he wants to accomplish. I'm only sorry that I never tried more of his cooking when I could've fully tasted it."

A pang in her chest. "Oh, I'm sorry." She reaches out and sets her hand on top of his.

Reflectively, Léon replies, "Yes, but we trade grief for more joy. For what opportunities I missed in my mortal life, there are hundreds I've had with the people dearest to me. We've defied grief, haven't we?"

Millie isn't so sure.

One day, I will die. Ezren might take a small piece with them, but we will both wither in time. All that'll be left are memories, like paintings.

"Sure. But it's still okay to miss certain things."

Léon processes what she's said, and then nods. "You're right. That's wise."

"I've been called a lot of things. I don't think that's one of them."

She blinks sluggishly, somehow both tired and more awake than ever. "I'm not sure what to do next." She puts the empty bowl on the plate and goes to stand, but Léon fluidly stands and reaches out, so she gives the dishes to him.

"Don't worry about the dishes, my witch. You can do what you want here. No need to worry. You look exhausted."

"I am."

"Do you want me to show you around? I could give you a proper tour."

Millie's worried if she stays any longer, he'll offer to carry her. Then again, the thought's not unappealing. "No, it's okay. I'd like to see for myself."

What are they? Friends? Lovers? Both? Or maybe the mine was just a situation that's passed, and they'll forget one another. They bonded over one stressful event.

He has two partners, after all; Millie is all for polyamory, but another partner would be awfully complicated for him, wouldn't it? Girlfriend and boyfriend feels like too much and not enough for what they went through in a remarkably short period.

And especially around someone as lovely as Claire...Millie's thoughts start to tumble into self-consciousness about how pretty Claire is, but it's not worry over her own appearance and how they compare, it's...her face gets hot.

She'll leave, maybe go back to live with Simon and Fel, and do...she doesn't know. The idea of making a future as an escaped convict hardens the pit of her stomach.

Millie jokes before they go their separate ways for the night, "I'll try not to break anything."

With his free hand, the dishes balanced in the other, Léon twirls a finger in his hair and gives her that mischievous, pearly-canined grin. "Oh, please do! It means we have an excuse to go shopping for new things. Matthias really doesn't go out browsing near enough."

Next, she finds herself alone. Not in the downstairs bedroom with its purple bed sheets and violet walls with spiraling vine designs, but a study that looks recently used, warm with a crackling fireplace and candles.

A lot of the manor is dark and gothic, but not gloomy.

She sits on one of the deep crimson sofas by the fire before stretching out and taking off her boots, which thunk softly on the carpet.

Millie can't keep her eyes open, so she doesn't fight sleep. Her shoulders sink into the tasseled pillow, and she dozes, her nose filled with the scents of smoke and tallow.

Her nap is peaceful and dreamless.

When Millie wakes up from her doze, she's bathed in enough warmth from the study fireplace for sweat to pool under her arms, and she's not alone anymore.

On the couch across from her, Claire sits and reads. Millie reaches out from under something that wasn't there before—a knitted blanket she hadn't pulled over herself, now draped over her shoulders.

I wonder if Léon made this.

As Millie stirs and shifts into a cross-legged sitting position, the other woman's green eyes fall on her. Claire is cross-legged, too, and wearing what Millie best describes as an immaculate, mauve pantsuit with pearls clinging to her throat.

Claire offers a kind smile. "Hello, I hope you don't mind."

I watched her revel in blood, and here we are.

Millie clears her throat, saying sheepishly, "I mean, yeah." Hastily, she corrects herself, "No, is what I mean. I don't mind. this is your home."

Don't be so meek.

"Yes. I imagine I could read somewhere else. I didn't know you were in here."

"I don't mind. Should *I* go?"

The vampire waves a hand. "No, no."

Millie rubs one eye with her palm, stray eyelashes falling on it. "What time is it?"

Claire sets her book aside. "About five in the morning."

Did Leon tell her that we kissed? Did he tell his boyfriend, too?

Boyfriend, husband, companion, she's not sure. Polygamy might not be legal, but that doesn't determine what people call each other.

Either way, she's not sure how open their relationship is. The idea makes her stomach cramp. Maybe all she ever will be is an outsider looking in. A solitary creature. An inconvenience. It might be sad, but there's a poetic ring to it.

"Wow, this is your casual reading wardrobe." Her cheeks flush. "Sorry, that sounded judgmental. I meant to sound impressed, because wow, you look really good, and I'm here in a shirt and boxers."

"Thank you. I suppose when you spend most of your time inside, one still wants to look dazzling even if not many see. At least, I do. We do."

"I see you for sure."

Claire laughs. "I'm always happy to have more people around. As we've grown content here, fewer people come by, and fewer stay. Not that I expect you to stay."

My heart is going crazy. She must hear it. I have to tell her more about the mines, if Léon hasn't already.

"Your husband and I..." Despite her determination to start, Millie can't find it in herself to finish.

"Yes, I know. We allow each other to do such things, to play, though normally, it never leads to anything substantial."

Normally.

Play. This doesn't feel like a game.

"I don't know what it means now. What we are to each other. But I really, really like him."

"I imagine you need time. You don't need to decide anything now. Simply rest and recover, and what will come will come."

"I had a request," she tells Claire.

"Of course. Anything for you."

Millie is taken aback, and she can't help the instinctive suspicion. "Anything? Wow. I'm not sure what to say."

Arm Languidly draped on the couch armrest, Claire bows her head. "I'm sorry. I don't mean to be so forward. You were with Léon when he needed help. I don't think Matthias and I can ever properly convey our appreciation, so I want to accommodate you as best I can."

Millie sets a hand on her full stomach. "I mean, you two have done a pretty good job." For a woman who was covered in blood when they first met, she finds Claire to be rather nice company. "Would it be possible for people to visit? Or, well, I'm not sure what'd be most discreet." Does this woman—Claire—know who she is?

"Of course, I'm sure it'd be possible to arrange that, so long as you aren't caught and arrested. Horrible, that." So, she does know.

Millie's voice is small. "I don't want to go back." She doesn't only mean prison.

"I'm sorry if I was making light."

"No, it's fine. You didn't say anything wrong."

"I don't know what it's like to be imprisoned, but I hope we can provide you with whatever you need to deal with whatever happened."

Millie's cheeks burn. She hates feeling indebted to anyone; when people give her these great, generous gifts she can never repay. Growing up, gifts were always conditional. *Be good or I'll return your Christmas presents.* "Thanks. I just..."

Claire waits for Millie to find what she wants to say.

"I have to let my friends know that I'm okay. It was shitty of me to just run off in the middle of the night. I, I've worried them sick because I couldn't face them." *Because I was so concerned about being a burden that I didn't care how I burdened them with fear. Maybe in the hopes that they'd let go.*

"I hear you," Claire says to Millie. Three simple words that feel like the world. "I'm sure they'll be elated to hear from you. But it might be better if one of us intercedes on your behalf, if you are truly still looked for by the law."

"Oh, I am, for sure. But it's not so bad, being wanted. Not everyone can say that."

"Indeed, though I don't see why they'd go through any strenuous effort to find you, since there are so many that have done far worse. Some might say what you did was admirable."

"Maybe admirable, still illegal. Probably could've killed me if I wasn't careful." Azoth is volatile, and even being in its proximity electrifies the air around it. Millie had no idea how it might affect her and her witch soul, except that she began having those strange firelight and sea dreams about Ezren, before she was caught, and except for a couple of nights, they drifted away like mist.

Claire is everything she isn't. Blonde and long-limbed and willowy and tall; meanwhile, Millie is short and tends toward the heavyset side, though she made peace with her body type a long time ago, mostly annoyed more so by the fragment of a demon inside her than her inability to lose much weight, even when Mom made her join in on those diets where she could only eat five-hundred calories a day and then got detention for sleeping in American history class.

Claire stands. A feeling stirs in Millie as she admires Claire's immortal exquisiteness, the jeweled shimmer of her green eyes, and she thinks the same thing she did in college when she first stared at another woman's nimble hands: *Do I want to be her, or kiss her?*

When Claire comes over, Millie sits up straight and instinctively leans forward.

"May I?" Claire asks. "Are you sure?"

Expecting a hug, Millie replies, "Yeah, go ahead. But be careful. I haven't brushed my teeth or used mouthwash for at least forty-eight hours." God, she can't wait to take a bath and get into bed.

With that, Claire leans down and kisses Millie on both cheeks, her perfume sweet but spicy, like cloves, or carnations.

The witch feels herself burn beet-red as Claire moves away with a reserved smile.

Right. A French thing. French people do the kiss on the cheek thing. She thinks. It doesn't mean anything. It's like a hug, but with lips. No, wait.

"If you're amenable to it," Claire tells her, "I look forward to spending more time together."

Earnestly, Millie replies, "Yeah. Me, too."

Chapter 12

When Simon and Fel meet Millie at the top of the impressive stone steps of the vampire manor, they crush her in a close three-person hug.

The scars on Millie's upper left arm sting, but she hugs them back.

When they pull away, Fel deeply frowns. "Oberon's tits, you know if something happened to you..."

Millie ducks her head. "I know. I'm sorry." Quick, too quick, she adds, "I wish I knew how to show you both that I appreciate you."

Simon sighs and shakes his head, patting Millie's elbow. "You don't need to prove anything. Not to me, anyway. I'm just glad that you're okay."

Fel sets one hand on her cocked hip. "Yeah, that's what's most important, *but*. Mills. Going out in the middle of the night when there are gaunts roaming around? Really?"

Millie explains, "I didn't want you to worry?" At Fel's other hand going to palm her face, she elaborates, "I'm going to try to not do stunts like that again. It felt logical at the time."

Simon stares up at a snarling wolf statue down on the nearest landing. "Okay, so I'm really curious. How exactly did you end up at the castle of a vampire lord? And that woman mentioned something about you saving someone?"

"Yeah, I ended up in the abandoned mines with Léon. He's also a vampire."

With an inquisitive dip in his brow, Simon tells her, "You know you're welcome at the house, but are you going to be staying here?"

"I'm...not really sure."

That evening, after her friends have gone, Millie finds herself in Matthias' greenhouse. At least, Leon has told her that Matthias is the primary user. She finds an array of herbs and flowers, including a rosebush with one wilted flower.

Raising a single finger, she gently pokes one of the browning wine-red petals. She takes a deep breath, and the fire flows out. But rather than a flame, the rose grows healthy, like blood and feeling flooding into a numb limb.

The door creaks open and she turns to find Matthias standing there, keeping his distance.

"Apologies," he says, "I was checking on them. I suppose I should've been more aware of your interest, given..."

Given your past that got you arrested unfairly.

Millie lowers her hand from the rose. "I actually wanted to talk to you."

His gaze is level, but she detects a hint of surprise. She seems to be evoking that a lot. "Me?"

"Uh, so I know this is your house and all..."

"Our house," Matthias corrects, unsmiling, hands behind his back, and when Millie meets those gray eyes, he elaborates, "Claire, Léon, and I have shared it since 1924."

She thinks about how Matthias, reserved and even a little cold toward her, let his guard down to rest his forehead against Léon's.

"Yeah. I should be going soon." She swallows thickly, looking him over. He really is quite handsome. Beautiful.

And then, with his hands clasped behind his back, the centuries-old vampire looks tired, or vaguely annoyed, or both. "I don't want to presume, but haven't you been running from location to location enough already?"

Millie never thought about it like that, being on the run. It was more like she stayed in one place and then got stuck in another because of a massive bat-monster. Oh, hell. Semantics.

The vampire lord opens his mouth, and then closes it. Measuring his words before he speaks.

Matthias says, "If you'd like to stay here with us, you can. Claire and Léon are more than amiable to the idea." Millie wonders who proposed it first.

Millie blinks. "Indefinitely?"

The vampire's face truly looks as if it's etched in stone for a few seconds. "I don't know. It could happen that way, or you might move on. I can't say. It would be safer here, given your status as an escaped convict. No one comes into my domain without answering to me." Matthias smooths a hand down the red, ruffled thing that reminds her of a turkey's wattle. An ascot? That's not it... "Besides, if you make Léon and Claire happy, I don't mind sharing the space."

Scratching the back of her head, she asks, "What would you need me to do? You know, around the house. Or anything, I guess."

Matthias replies, "I don't want anything from you, though I would hope that you would impart some of your alchemical knowledge to me, so we could perhaps work on a cure for the gaunt affliction. Otherwise, don't cause a mess." He pauses, casting a glance to a crumpled pile of clothes in the corner near the nightstand. "Any more messes." Despite what he's giving her, his tone is wintry.

She keeps from indignantly stating that, obviously, she was going to pick those up and put them into the washer. Wherever the laundry room was. Vampires doing laundry. Huh. Well, Matthias cooks, and cleans, so it's not that much of a stretch.

"I can try...with my friends' help, with my new power, I can try to learn how to cast a glamor when I go out. To make things even safer."

"That would be advisable. I'm sure the others would love to shop with you, too, and If you need any clothes mended, Léon or I can help." This is a little more conversational than he was before.

Leon has mentioned shopping a few times...Millie has never been one to browse and go out shopping, but well, if the vampires have money, and she needs stuff, it might be nice to get out and just...have fun. With no expectation. Huh. What a weird feeling.

"Oh, thanks. What about Claire?"

He takes a step forward, nearer to her left side, so his voice sounds a little off. "She's excellent at stitching wounds. I'm not sure about clothes." Brusquely, he adds, "I can manage that, if need be."

"Nice. I'll keep that in mind. I used some moss I altered on my cuts. And Léon's." She still flinches when her palm ghosts over her shoulder, remembering the new scars, just like the old ones. Best to remind herself that scars are better than being a pile of flesh-ribbons.

"We appreciate what you did for him," Matthias tells her, still so stiff and formal. "What do you prefer to eat?"

"I don't know. I eat a lot of poultry and seafood, I guess. Pasta. I like pasta. Um. Can vampires eat garlic?"

"I would not eat it, but I can cook with it."

"I can't hear well out of my left ear," she tells the Count. "It's easier to hear you on my right side."

Though he maintains the space between them, he moves to her other side.

Once again, he avoids eye contact. Millie gets it; it wasn't until high school, when students and teachers would rib her for never meeting anyone's eyes and just staring ahead, that she forced herself to look at others. She doesn't press him.

Again, Matthias hesitates, raising both hands to rub a palm over his knuckles. "I am simply used to things being a certain way for decades. But I became accustomed to being alone for centuries, and then I grew used to having them in my life, my fires of my heart. Their jokes, their laughter. I will grow used to this change." He blinks, and as if remembering something he's forgotten, his eyes fall on her. "I don't mean to be..."

Millie shakes her head and shuffles her feet. "It's okay. I'm not really good with social stuff either."

He huffs a laugh. "Who said I was terrible at being social?"

She shares her own unsmile, and she feels like, one day, they might bridge this gap.

Too soon, his demeanor grows serious again. All business. "Why do you care about the gaunts?"

There's something about those steely gray eyes that haunts her. Haunts him. She wonders if he'll ever tell her.

"They're seen as disposable now, but not to me. They're people, and even if I don't know the reason why this change is happening to them so rapidly, I'll find the solution. They deserve it."

His brow grows taut, and his gaze flashes with pain. The kind a memory brings. He gives a nod, looks down at his boots, as dark as his long, gray coat.

With nothing else to say, he bows his head and walks out.

"Your brow is set in a serious manner," Leon teases, taking Millie's hand.

"Sorry I don't have clothes besides what Simon and Fel brought." And nothing so...*fancy* and gothic. With chiffon and frilly lace, and the cravats! "I was just thinking about what to do." Will she be able to get an online job or something? Probably not, and she also likely won't be able to complete her degree, after she dropped out with two semesters left. Now, that's a kick in the dick.

Léon shoots a feline grin to Claire: "Are you thinking what I am?"

Millie blinks, not liking their shared slyness, the hint of a scheme as prevalent as the rosy perfume in the air. "What?"

Following the both of them down a narrow sidewalk, she stuffs her tingling fingers into her jacket pockets. Red and green tinsel and blinking Christmas lights twinkle on streetlights and shops.

Léon is saying, "We should really go out and buy things more often. It's a shame Matthias doesn't enjoy these things."

Claire reminds him, "You know how practical he is."

"He sees microwaves as frivolous. The man drinks his blood cold." Leon shudders.

Millie looks at herself in a shop window, the her-not-her that fills her with unease. Besides her lack of potent power in her college days, she resisted the desire to find a way to use glamors because she knew she'd want to make herself skinnier, and to finally have hair that wouldn't make her mom *tsk* and chide, "You really should straighten your hair more. It looks so much better that way."

Millie asks them, "Does Matthias always clean the entire place alone?"

Claire tells her, "Not always. He likes doing it, so we let him do it alone if he wishes."

Léon waves a hand. "I've offered to help, but he was insistent. Even when I offered to dress up as a maid!"

Millie guesses that when you're a vampire, you're eternally alone with your thoughts. She doesn't want that; she was told that certain witches can live until they're two-hundred years old, maybe longer.

Claire explains some more, "He can be very solitary at times, so it's important that we let him be alone when he needs to be. He will come around when he's comfortable."

Millie nods in understanding, as Leon points to one of the shops and says to them, "Come, this place has some lovely coats."

They spend over an hour weaving through stores and collecting bags in the darkening twilight.

Eventually, Leon goes inside to chat with the owner of a used bookstore while Claire peruses a shelf outside of some of the free offers, which mostly consists of encyclopedias from decades prior.

"So, I didn't want to pry," Millie starts.

"Pry away. I'll let you know if I don't want to speak about something."

Claire's voice is both smooth as honey and gentle as a breeze, but it sometimes dips in a raspy contralto that makes Millie's heart skip a beat. The cadence of an ocean-dream.

"Léon is with both of you. How do you feel about Matthias?"

Claire fans her hand along the tops of some used textbooks. "I like Matthias. He's a steady presence. We respect each other. I don't think he and I have what he and Léon have, or what Léon and I have, but that's all right. I enjoy being with him. When you're with him, you feel as if you're the only person in the world. He listens."

"You don't ever get jealous? You don't ever worry about being locked out of the relationship, where it's just them and not you?"

"Never. We all trust one another."

Despite Claire's confidence, she can't help but detect a lingering...sadness? Not toward Leon or Matthias, but in general. Not too surprising that an immortal person might get melancholy. Vampires can sleep, but they don't need to, and the idea of being with your thoughts twenty-four/seven...

Millie doesn't know if a literal place called Hell exists, but if it did, it'd be a quiet, cold room where her thoughts play out without pause.

I'm so different from all of them. I look so different. I don't have their grace. And she must eat and sleep and go to the bathroom. She worries about silly things, like what they must think of her when she spills water on her shirt or passes gas or listens to "Living Dead Girl" or "Queen of Winter, Throned" twelve times in a row at four in the morning. She hasn't put on "Funeral in Carpathia" though. She's wondered if Matthias might be sensitive to that one.

She wonders if she'll have to continue to nap during the day to see them; mostly, she's always been a night owl, but school and her job at the bookstore warehouse demanded that she be awake from eight in the morning to ten at night.

Whose expectations do you really have to follow here?

Millie lets her arms fall to her sides.

They don't want anything from you. You don't need to impress them.

When her attention is on Claire again, the other woman's eyes are hooded in contemplation.

"Everything okay?" Millie inquires.

"Yes. I don't mean to disparage your glamor. It's quite impressive magic, but I certainly prefer your true face."

Well. Damn.

Millie's face burns. She hopes that doesn't translate to her false mask. Already, Claire has a way of intuiting her mood and knowing when to linger and when to gently break her melancholy.

As they all saunter down the street like anyone else, Millie swallows thickly, trying to blink the sting in her eyes away. "Thanks. Thanks for being so nice."

"Of course." Claire pauses, and then repeats, "Of course. There's no need to thank me for that."

This woman could break me with her pinkie, and maybe I'd like it way too much.

Millie had never had many friends, but when she did, they were always guys because she always felt pressure to prove that unlike other girls she was smart and brazen. She'd chastise her own stupidity now, but everyone encouraged that thought process, even her mom, who straddled the fence of "I was a tomboy when I was your age" and "but I realized I had to act like a proper lady eventually, and you should learn, too." Her same mom who said "all men are perverts" and "boys will be boys," all the same, preferred that her daughter loathed her own womanhood because, in that manner, they were alike, and there could be control there.

No trust in other women, and, really, no trust in anyone.

Both views made the idea of companionship with women restrictive. Either she'd suppress or lose herself. Every way she expressed herself was wrong. It's not that she ever doubted her womanhood, but she doubted her ability to ever fit into a box without disappointing someone or causing conflict, and she was never sure of the line between envying another woman and wanting to sleep with her.

She looks at Claire and tentatively returns her earnest smile. Maybe it'll be nice to have another woman as a friend.

As they talk, two men walk past and stop near them, one in an unbuttoned, gray suit jacket and a white collared shirt.

He says to his companion, who looks into the bookstore window, "You know, there are more police officers around."

His friend says, "Apparently, outside of town, there was a prison riot a few nights ago, and a couple of people escaped. Even a witch! They haven't been able to catch anyone yet."

"Oh, that's just great. We have a quiet little town here, and just imagine if there were more people from outside of town, especially criminals."

"We've only been here for ten months," his companion replies.

"Still! I'm practically a local, not like these urban tourists with their shitty city music. Can you imagine if we bumped into an escaped drug dealer? I'm already so used to checking if my wallet's there back in Atlanta."

Not able to help herself, Millie snaps, "I'd rather bump into a drug dealer than a prejudiced asshole with bad cologne."

The man sneers at her. "Excuse you, stranger, but I got my degree in African-American literature from Stanford, thank you very much. One of my favorite books is *The Bluest Eye*. What would a redneck know about anything?"

Then, the man drives his fist into his own cheek. He spits out a stream of blood, and then does it again, punching and slapping himself. He stumbles down the sidewalk, his companion trying to steady him and make his arm stop.

Claire hasn't once taken her eyes off the clothes rack when she says to Millie, "Don't worry. I won't kill him."

"Yeah, I guess killing would be rude." Millie doesn't so much mind Claire doing this for her, but she worries that others might suspect that *Millie* is doing it, and they might guess far more than they should.

Although, if they're used to vampires...

Claire sniffs, arching her chin primly. "*He* was rude. He should consider it a courtesy." As if sensing Millie's worry over being discovered, Claire's expression softens. "I'm sorry to stress you. Let's go." She looks into the bookstore and catches Leon's eye, and he comes to follow them.

"You know," he tells Claire, "I really miss all the fun when I start chattering."

"Hey," Millie says, touching Claire's elbow as slaps and concerned chatter rings in the background. "Thanks. Seriously."

God. Léon is beautiful and kind and funny and wonderful, but Claire is...Millie doesn't even know if the word exists. She's scary in a way that doesn't frighten Millie at all.

Claire's mouth dips into a somber frown, as if noticing Millie's thoughts from the look in her eyes—the only available reflection. "Don't get your hopes up with me. I am not quite a good person, as you've seen."

Millie knows she isn't always perfect, but she also knows that she doesn't agree with the idea that the best people do nothing. Are just nice, but not kind.

"I thought you were pretty badass, actually."

The other woman's eyelashes flutter. "Thank you."

Millie looks at a painting outside of her new bedroom, a lighthouse with a small house beside it

She points at the art. "This is a nice painting."

Beside her, Claire smiles serenely. "You flatter me. I did it."

"Really? Did you do all the paintings in the manor?"

"Most of them. In life, I never had much space or time for painting, but that changed when we met Matthias. Léon has his knitting and crocheting; Matthias has his science and cooking; I have my paintings."

Millie finds herself rubbing a hole into the back of her head. "Neat. I draw sometimes, but I never painted much. I write sometimes, went to school for it. But that's about it."

"I'd love to read anything you've written."

"Oh. Thanks. It's just, none of my workshops liked my stuff, so I haven't done it as much."

"Were you allowed to write in prison?"

"Yeah, I had a journal, but I just felt..." She can't describe it entirely. Gray. Like half-watered grits, where you take a bite and crunch the dusty grains and grimace, but tell yourself you're still being fed.

"I'd like to read something of yours one day. But first, it's all right to take a break and adjust." She makes it sound like she understands. God, at some point, Claire has died. Yeah, Millie can imagine needing to take time to adjust after a trauma like that. "In the past, when I don't have as much melancholy, I'll offer to do painting classes in prison. Perhaps you and I could do painting and writing classes for prisoners. Of course, I know it would be a great ordeal for you to try something like that."

"Sure. It's a good idea. I want to, you know, give something to people. What they deserve to have. Maybe I'll be ready one day."

Claire agrees with a soft smile that makes Millie's heart flutter. "In time, perhaps." And that's when Millie is aware of the tautness in the center of her brow

Millie wishes that, like Claire lets her art take up space, she could let go of her worries over her writing. Maybe sharing her writing is the first step. well. The first step is writing something that isn't her journal, back in the prison, probably chunked in the trash with all the tears and stray eyelashes between the pages.

Right next to a leering gargoyle statue in the living room, Léon sits on a stool and is busy shifting fabrics around and doing something with his cricut. He's wearing a breezy, sky-blue dress that accentuates his lithe arms and shoulders; the front laces and little bow at his throat arc undone. The space below her stomach stirs.

When he sees her approaching, he flicks the cricut with a finger. "Oh, hello, Millie. Don't mind me. Just trying to get this device to do what I want it to do."

Millie glances over his neat stack of knitted creations, a pastel rainbow of hats, socks, cozies, and more. "Hey, I can put a warming charm on those things you make for kids. it's just a small little magic touch."

"Thank you. That would be delightful. Oh, before I forget. This is your color, so I must insist that you have it." He picks up a violet hat that even has that silly little ball on the top, his thumbs slipped into the hollow and displaying it to her as a gift. "You don't have to wear it, of course."

Millie gazes at the purple winter hat, and she accepts it, taking it in her hands and feeling the wool, both coarse and soft, on her palms, and then, as her eyes sting with hot tears—

She sets the hat carefully on the nearby coffee table, and she must look glum as tears fall and Léon pauses in concern, raising an unsure hand.

With a sharp inhale, Millie wraps her arms around him, digging her fingers into the back of his tunic. He smells of vanilla, roses, wood, and tallow, of the stone tomb below. He rubs his fingers soothingly into the middle of her back.

In an unfurnished, lonely room, Millie palms a silver cross that dangles from the neck of a statue of a forlorn woman with her hands clasped in prayer.

"It's that Catholic guilt, you know?"

Leaning against the entrance with his arms crossed, Léon offers a veiled smile that doesn't match his eyes. "Oh, I know."

Around dawn, Millie dreams of a strange man with blonde hair, deep blue eyes, and pointed ears driving a stake through her heart, and she wakes up screaming.

On her back, she shuts her mouth, her heart rapidly beating. She sucks deep breaths through her nose. The first image she imagines is the lighthouse, like the broken one on the island nearby, but with the stream of moonish light. Claire's painted lighthouse. Or Ruth, sad Ruth waiting for Naomi.

"Millie?"

Speak of the vampire. She sits up to see both Claire and Léon standing at the door—her door.

They have matching gowns, she realizes. She's reminded of old movies and the three brides of Dracula in wisps of white.

Claire clasps her hand to her chest, staying at the door, while Leon enters when she gives him a nod.

The other woman says so softly, "We heard you scream and wanted to check on you."

"Nightmare," she explains, clasping the sheets to her black sweatshirt. "It was...it was...it hurt," she manages.

Leon comes and sits at the end of her bed, setting an elegant hand on the sheets. "Do you want me to stay?"

She's touched by their concern, but ah, there it is, that urge to send them away, to say she'll be fine seizes her, but worse is the guilt when she knows she wants them to stay.

Entitled. Presumptuous. Selfish. Do vampires even sleep in beds? They call the coffins their beds.

It's okay. You're safe and warm. She tells Ezren that as, thrumming and vibrating, they coil against her ribcage like a cat near a heater.

She wonders if Claire and Léon can hear the angel inside her. The fire, the hum, and sometimes, that soft knell like wind chimes. She'll have to ask.

Once, during the day, Millie went down the stairs she found in the corner of the living room, half-hidden by a four-paneled partition of woven wood. evoking a fire in the center of her palm, she went down the hard steps and found a small cross-shaped room of stones. in each of the three squared points of the area were coffins, are coffins. Well, more like fancy caskets of polished wood and metal. Flames, big and small, danced against the iron and gold.

The one at the end, where torches blazed, was painted black and bigger, made to fit more than one or two people. Not that the other caskets were small by any means. She'd guessed the black and iron one was Matthias', and that despite its austere look, it was the official cuddle time coffin.

The coffin to the right, vibrant gold-lined cherrywood, had a sketchpad and a few books, where Claire might get up to doodle, and the one to the left, white and lined with rose gold, had some yarn and needles, so Leon might knit. Matthias had nothing, and in the center were three armchairs surrounded by standing candelabras. She imagines the three of them finding solace and peace in the dark, just chatting away about the past.

She'd rapped on the one that was obviously Leon's, stepping back when he groggily raised the lid and, after they shared a glance, without a word, he shifted to let her into the plush, golden interior, which was much comfier and roomy than she anticipated. His grin was a bit sheepish, and though he was sleeping alone in the simple, lacy white gown of a gothic heroine on a pulp novella cover, she caught the scent of a sharper cologne and the crimson lipstick stains on his face.

"I don't want to take up too much space," she said.

"Some days we all share Matthias' bed," Leon had confessed, "But I don't want you to be cramped."

She got in.

With the casket lid open, she rested her head on his chest, and she had to admit it was cozy.

Now, in the bed, Millie tells both Claire and Leon:

"Yeah, I think I need someone to stay with me tonight. Please stay." When Claire sets her hand on the door and looks as if she might step out and leave them, she clarifies, "Both of you." A pause. She holds Claire's pensive but surprised look. There's a more tender emotion there that she's too tired to place. "If you want."

It's bold, maybe too bold, but the other woman gives her a gentle smile and nod.

So, they come to her.

Millie lies on her side, between Claire and Leon. *I guess this means Matthias is sleeping alone.* That makes her feel a little bad.

Maybe they all heard her scream, and Matthias told them that they could go. Despite not knowing her well, and despite her not quite slipping past his armor, he put her before himself.

With Léon nuzzled against her back, Millie slips her hand into Claire's, and in the tangle of arms and hair and the distant song of ocean waves, she sleeps warmly, dreamlessly.

About the Author

Morgan is a horror, fantasy, and romance author. They have a soft spot for all things dark and gothic, especially vampires and an array of castle-dwelling monsters. They've also never written an angel that they didn't want to make at least a little weird-looking. They live in the Southern United States with a menagerie of ill-behaved cats and dogs, including a malevolent tortoiseshell named Satan. More about their work can be found at morgandante.com.

www.ingramcontent.com/pod-product-compliance
Lightning Source LLC
Chambersburg PA
CBHW071523170626
46811CB00007B/2936